TRAI

Sometimes my new Little Master loves me so much he licks me all over my cheeks and ears. Nibbles, too. The big one tells him, "We don't do that." But the little one does it anyway.

They train us, me and my little one, at the same time. "Tight but light," the big one says to him. "Remember your hand strength."

Our trainer sits on a high stool and watches. He carries a pole long enough to reach the whole round pen. Then he starts to yell—at my Little Master, even though he's His Excellent Excellency About-To-Be-The-Ruler-Of-Us-All.

"Look! Look! Remember every Sam can tell which way to turn by your own head movements. Poke him! Poke! Poke! Far side! If you got poked in one side, which way would *you* move? Give him a pat. He's done well. But never pat for no good reason."

I get tired of hearing the exact same thing every day, but my Little Master has to learn. They yell at him a lot more than they yell at me. They always say if the rider is good then the mount is good.

But my Little Master, The Future-Ruler-Of-Us-All, is still too young to be masterful.

FIREBIRD
WHERE SCIENCE FICTION SOARS™

THE
MOUNT

Carol Emshwiller

FIREBIRD
AN IMPRINT OF PENGUIN GROUP (USA) INC.

FIREBIRD
Published by the Penguin Group
Penguin Group (USA) Inc., 345 Hudson Street, New York, New York 10014, U.S.A.
Penguin Group (Canada), 10 Alcorn Avenue, Toronto, Ontario, Canada M4V 3B2
(a division of Pearson Penguin Canada Inc.)
Penguin Books Ltd, 80 Strand, London WC2R 0RL, England
Penguin Ireland, 25 St Stephen's Green, Dublin 2, Ireland (a division of Penguin Books Ltd)
Penguin Group (Australia), 250 Camberwell Road, Camberwell, Victoria 3124, Australia
(a division of Pearson Australia Group Pty Ltd)
Penguin Books India Pvt Ltd, 11 Community Centre,
Panchsheel Park, New Delhi - 110 017, India
Penguin Group (NZ), Cnr Airborne and Rosedale Roads, Albany, Auckland,
New Zealand (a division of Pearson New Zealand Ltd)
Penguin Books (South Africa) (Pty) Ltd, 24 Sturdee Avenue, Rosebank,
Johannesburg 2196, South Africa

Registered Offices: Penguin Books Ltd, 80 Strand, London WC2R 0RL, England

First published in the United States of America by Small Beer Press, 2002
Published by Firebird, an imprint of Penguin Group (USA) Inc., 2005

1 3 5 7 9 10 8 6 4 2

LIBRARY OF CONGRESS CATALOGING-IN-PUBLICATION DATA
Emshwiller, Carol.
The mount / Carol Emshwiller.
p. cm.
ISBN 0-14-240302-4 (pbk.)
1. Human-alien encounters—Fiction. 2. Human beings—Fiction.
3. Young men—Fiction. I. Title.
PS3555.M54M68 2005   813'.54—dc22   2004056341

Printed in the United States of America

To Michael Kandel

Thank you for believing in it and helping in so many ways.

Chapter One

We're not against you, we're for. In fact we're built for you and you for us—we, so our weak little legs will dangle on your chest and our tail down the back. Exactly as you so often transport your own young when they are weak and small. It's a joy. Just like a mother-walk.

You'll be free. You'll have a pillow. You'll have a water faucet and a bookcase. We'll pat you if you do things fast enough and don't play hard to catch. We'll rub your legs and soak your feet. Sams and Sues, and you Sams had better behave yourselves.

You still call us aliens in spite of the fact that we've been on your world for generations. And why call aliens exactly those who've brought health and happiness to you? And look how well we fit, you and us. As if born for each other even though we come from different worlds.

We mate the stocky with the stocky, the thin with the thin, the pygmy with the pygmy. You've done a fairly good job with that yourselves before we came. As to skin, we like a color a little on the reddish side. Freckles are third best.

1

Your type is called a Seattle. I hope to find other Seattles to mate with you, and soon.

Your young will stay with their mothers until weaning. We'll stroke them all over to make them love us. Four months is the crucial time for imprinting you predators. And your young do love us. You all do. We're the ones with the treats. Leather straps will help keep you in line and help us keep our seat. There will sometimes be prickers on our toes. How and if these are used, and when, depends, of course, on *you*.

You are the recipient of our kindness, our wealth and knowledge, our intelligence, our good growth of greens. Without us you'd not exist. Remember that. Though it's true a few of you still survive in the mountains. We care nothing for mountains. What can you grow in the mountains that's not better grown in the valleys? Or build?

There is no need for you, or any of you, to learn how to count. And why read? We like you well-muscled. Reading is not conducive to muscles. We prefer that you hook yourself to the go-round instead.

My offspring will be pleased with you. They already know good lines: Slope of shoulders, rise of chest, slim waist, more so in your females. And, and most important, sturdy legs. Legs are what we're taught to notice first. Hands last. Compared to ours, your hands are so small and weak. Then there's the look in the eye. You should have a kind eye. Many things depend on such knowledge, or else there would be more danger than there already always is.

Our young adore you. They even adore your straps and buckles. They keep your pictures above where they curl up.

They hang your worn-out shoes over their doorways. They save apples for you that they feed you piece-by-piece—and strawberries and chocolate.

As we go along on your shoulders, head to head (so sweetly!), cheek to cheek, our sun hats cover you also, and our rain hats. Some of us whisper our most secret secrets into your ear as we go.

Though I have prods and poles, I believe in explaining. Even to you, though you are as children. I believe it is safer that you understand—at least in part. You will never *fully* understand, but you must trust us, that we *always* have our reasons.

So I speak. "Tomorrow I will attach you to a circling line. You will be strapped up for the journey after the friskiness is taken out of you." We prefer that there be no fight left and no ideas.

There are reasons for all this—all this from the start, I mean, and how we came to be on top. First, of course, there's the fact that we're superior in every way. You should be happy to serve such as we. And we can tell if you're not. We have studied diagrams of your facial expressions. We can read your forehead and your lips, the wrinkles at the outsides of your eyes. Do not squint. It is unsightly.

You have a good life here. And, and most important, you are free—free in your stalls for a part of every day. You may rest and recuperate. If you have a book, and know how, you can read.

This is a case of prey over predator. You must admit, it's only fair. Since we are prey, we can see, as you might put it, around corners, though that is not true. We simply see behind as well as in front. We know when a bug moves in a bush.

Now is the time for the willingness that is in you, since you are bred for it. We count on you for crossing whatever needs to be crossed without hesitation. Try to look good as you do it. Sweep ahead and don't glance to the side. It's our job to do the seeing. If danger lurks, *we* will let you know when to beware—when to jump back—when to turn around and run. Our senses are keener and we judge better than you can. A little tickle on the ear . . . *you* could decide on that as the signal. The choice is yours, of course. You are free. After our trip we'll give you a good rubdown and lots of pats. (*We* like strokes—it reminds us of the lickings of our ancestors—but *you* like pats, so thinking only of you, we'll pat.)

And so we will enter the forest. Those of your kind who might be hiding there are few and should not be a trouble.

Already my heart is with your heart. We are two of one single kind, companions about to take a companionable outing. Surely as much fun for you as for me.

The meaning of life, yes, yes, and of butterflies. You would say they are two separate questions. We say they're the same one.

"Wake up. It's time. Kneel. This sack isn't heavy. You'll hardly notice it. Turn to your near side so I may mount. Near, I say. Near, near, *near!*"

Enter the forest. Appreciate the trees. Sure-footed friend. The ground is rough. My balance will help to hold you steady. When have I ever fallen, even when mounted on the very young? And here you are at the peak of your strength.

Oh, a day like this! One mountain would be enough, yet here are many. A dozen flowers, a dozen butterflies are all I would ask for, yet here are many dozens. And you, swinging along so lively, as if as new as the day.

Trust me, that I will lead us to a happy meadow where there will be a stream. Then I will give you a treat. "Have you your comb? My kind sees all sides and could be anywhere. I want you to look good."

The social consequences of the journey must be taken into consideration. There is the mess that may inadvertently be made, if, that is, we encounter any of them—your sort. Should we see any, we will be obligated to round them up and bring them in, out of kindness and for their own safety. (That's the reason for this pole.) The forest is cruel and dangerous, and there are no medical services available. It's a wonder you survive there, those few of you that do. I've heard you eat acorns and the roots of Solomon Seal.

So, "Go, go, go!"

We go.

Trot and again trot, and I, by the motion of the stepping . . . I, as if having jumped back into the womb as I used to love to do. In those days any womb would do. Lulled, therefore, into a half-sleep—a half-dream—of mothers. We follow a paved way towards a mountain, though we'll turn before we get there.

Pat your shoulder. "Good boy." Praise is better than punishment.

"Don't be afraid of the river. I know this river. One such as you can cross it easily. You're a heavy and a tall. That's why I chose you. Your head will be above it. See if it isn't. Even my toes will stay dry. See if they aren't.

"Cross the river, shake out. Comb your hair. Isn't that refreshing?"

"Go, go, go along and go along. Knees high. Head up. Points off for slouching. I have a thought to feature you." I would be much admired if you were high-stepping and had your hair slicked up and out. "Up and out, chest also. Chin in."

The morning is so sweet I will sing of it and of love. "La, la, la, love. Lee, la, love." And of you, my sturdy. We haven't been together long, but you will know how I love you already.

Keep on. The work of the world is always done by creatures too tired to do it.

"Jump that log." I will lean forward to help. "Lovely, lovely." (Pat, pat, pat.) All so far, and the world, and the ways of it. "Be happy."

Hear. Our ears are better. See, smell. Ours are better. How could we not have come to be your masters? Let us show you the way. From sun to shade to sun again, to shade. They say you cannot even smell the sun.

"Go," I say out loud. "And go," I say.

Here the remains of a primitive fire. I pull you to the side around it. I cover your eyes. "Go, my steady. Go, go. Well done." (Pat, pat, pat.) "We'll not rest until another length or so."

That way you'll be too tired to notice if another primitive fire spot turns up.

And it does. And another. I cover your eyes each time. Perhaps we've lost our way. I drop my hands from your eyes as if scales after moltings. I let my hands hover around your throat. It's as a warning. "Peace," I say. "We have always been peaceful creatures, as you well know. And you also, peaceful creatures, too."

Down a steep bank, you, slipping and sliding. I don't want any mud on me or my whites. I pull, this side and that. You throw your head as if to escape my pulling. You grunt. Thank goodness you have been well-trained in not making inappropriate noises.

"Good job. Did you hurt yourself?"

You know better than to answer.

I have two spots of mud. Best be uncomplaining. That's always peaceable.

A stream. And another. A place where it's hard to push through the brush. I wish I'd thought of your leggings. I don't want unsightly scratches on your legs.

Perhaps we really are lost. I have my fix-upon and here is a good place to separate myself from you.

"Kneel. Near side. Near! Near! Are you listening, or don't you yet know your near from your far? Hush. You know better than to answer. Some of you never seem to be able to learn near from far. Why is that? Hush. You know better than to speak."

This is a good time for a treat. One bite. You don't smell well enough to know I have lots more.

"You may squat."

"Here is a sip and a bite."

I love to watch your muscles. I love to see you move with the spots of sun shining down.

But I'm tired, I will mount again and rest on your warmth. Let me look at you first . . . again and yet again. The shine of you with sweat! What a magnificent creature!

"Near. Near!" And, "Go, go, go. My steady. Hurry."

But what can you know of time, poor, dear creature? Though many's the time I wish I had your notion of it.

Somebody watches. My better ears, my better nose. . . . *You* don't know. I'm sorry for your kind and your dull senses. I will do my best to keep you safe.

You shake your head. You thrust your elbows out and back. I suppose the straps bother you. I say, "Next stop I'll look at those straps. Hurry now. The faster we go, the sooner we stop. That's always the way." I don't say, but I want to get rid of the watchers. There is now more than one.

"Save your breath. Save your muscles. We'll rest at the next knob. Trust me." I say that last in case you, also, are aware of watchers. I say, "I have your best interests at heart. Without you, happy and healthy and strong, where would I be?"

Here by myself, helpless on my wobbly legs, but I don't say that.

"I count on your good will," I say, and, "We are *all* free, as you well know."

We should have turned long ago. I had not meant to get this close to the mountains. We're climbing. Is that your fault? Did you miss a turn on purpose? Perhaps you're a Wild? One who knows the mountains? You've been branded as Tame. You were stable-raised. I chose you specifically for your lineage—a long line of Seattle heavies. But there are some of us who are unscrupulous. Who change brands and lineage. Therefore you may be someone else entirely.

I unfold my pole. I spark it, one spark on each side and two in back.

Next knob.

"You may squat, my steady."

I dismount. I will sit here and sing. "La, la, low, lee." I'll save fear for another time, another place. My mothers told me that, and it stands me in good stead. Oh, the memory of mothers!

I say out loud, "I will sing, yet again, of love."

You are not, as a group, mean-spirited. Hardly ever. Perhaps they, hiding there (of your kind, if such they be), will feel sympathy when they hear my song. But your ears hear coarsely and cannot fathom overtones and undertones to any great extent. I suppose none of you will be able to tell anything important about an important song.

I hear them. They pretend to be birds. Do they think we can't tell? You silly, *sillies*, with your childish games.

"*Ho*. And yet again, *Ho*." And, "What a beautiful day." Snap of my pole here and there. Spark a tree. Spark a bush. Spark as if a star overhead. You flinch. You shy. Have you been mistreated?

I ask you out loud then. "Have you been mistreated? You may nod."

But you do not. You look away. You have an air of listening. We have become adept at reading your faces: The furrows of your frowns, the rictus of your smiles, but we also know sometimes you frown when you're puzzled, and sometimes when you turn up your mouth it is not a pleasant thing.

"If you've been mistreated, I'm sorry if such is the case."

I really *am* sorry. Such treatment is unforgivable when another creature is entrusted to our care. Can such as that breed trust and affection?

"Let me see the marks, if marks there be." Though there need be none. We have our ways. Also we never want to spoil a perfect body with ugly scars. Yours has scars, but it is especially perfect even so.

Things are there behind the underbrush, tweeting.

"Ho!" Ho is not a word we use when speaking to you. It resembles go, but you are able to distinguish between them.

I stand up to my full height. Our legs wobble, and standing straight takes willpower, but it's important at a moment like this one might become. But size and legs aren't everything, as look at us, you and me. Which rides the other?

Such a thing should stay in my thoughts. I don't say it. I remind myself: Be kind.

"See the berries? You may pick yourself a treat."

They will see my kindness. And I will take this opportunity to watch your muscles as you move. It's always a pleasure and a reassurance.

I'll curl up for a while, though I prefer to do my resting with my legs crossed across your chest, and when you are full of mother motions, back-and-forthing on the trail.

I will tell you again what a good and noble steady you are— noble eye and noble brow. A look of circumstance regardless of the circumstances. I will tell you this out loud.

"I said pick, and if you have the urge to lie down, you may, as long as you do not crease the surcingle."

Now a warm wind. "Rest, my sturdy steady, and let your sweat dry."

That I say out loud. "Rest. You may pick flowers or pick up feathers if you're so inclined." I know the simple pleasures of your kind.

"Are you happier out here among the trees, my faithful? If so, we'll come from time to time. You may nod."

But your only answer is to show your noble profile as you listen still. (I would have preferred your nose be not quite so long. Perhaps it can be fixed. But I did not choose you for your face.) You haven't even picked a berry. Perhaps we do wrong in teaching you silence, though I've heard that if we don't, you do nothing but chatter and squawk.

And here, suddenly, a female of your kind. A Sue, partly hidden in the scrub willow. Stringy and muscular, but not at all as muscular as you, and definitely not another Seattle. Her hair is neither black nor blond nor red but a nondescript in-between. She's a freckled and I would guess badly sunburned. No wonder the freckled are third best.

Why would she suddenly appear? And at such a time as this? I pretend I don't notice, though you must know I do, since I always notice everything before you. When have I ever not?

'Tis said, The happier the creature, the less to fear.

I say out loud, "Do you have a love life—a wishful mating of your own determination? Something could be arranged. You may speak."

I unfold my pole.

No answer.

"Your hair. See to your hair."

No answer. Perhaps he is mute. I've heard that some of you, when trained for silence too brutally, lose your voices altogether. (Silence is important for many reasons. Your kind has a tendency to have ideas.)

Not only no answer, but you haven't combed yourself, either.

The female stands so still I have a hard time picking her out when I look again, though I know she's there. I smell her. She's wearing a sort of sack thing exactly the same color as bark and leaves. But she has it belted with silver links from fancy old surcingles. That is a mistake unless one wants to be noticed. I presume she wants her waist to be noticed.

Her hair is not combed nor has it any shine.

I say, "Beware." I point the pole at her.

Something will happen because this Sam is a brave and noble creature. He would save her at his own expense.

She speaks. She calls him Heron. I had been told his name is Beauty.

You finally notice. I can tell your smile is a real smile this time.

What would happen if everybody mated with everybody else? I shudder at the thought. We don't stoop to that. It has been said, if you were let loose, there would be nothing but chaos.

"Would you like me to find you a mate?" I say.

And then, "We are two of one kind. Comrades in mutual admiration."

Then I say, and I say it firmly, "One way to live is *not* as good as another."

But the self will know another of its own kind. The self will see its other self in another self's eyes. This can't be helped.

The Sue talks too much. As do all your kind. Even if you could hear as well as we do, how could you hear when you're always chittering? I see how she is healthy in spite of how she must live out here. I don't want to think about it, the dirty food and the raw, or, on the other hand, the burnt. Can there ever be anything—even one thing— really white in a place like this?

And now here comes another one, a Sam this time. Not a handsome one. Not like you, my steady. His chest is narrow and concave. He hasn't even the look of a sprinter. You must be more than twice his weight. I would pit you against him and watch you win. Though sometimes the Sues fight alongside their Sams.

Why is this Sue calling you Heron? What is the meaning of that with reference to the past, and what does that portend?

Well, now and now. Look. See what you do. You are removing your harness as easily as can be, as if it had never been buckled behind your back where none of you can reach. You whistle. I have heard that tune before. It is simple, as everything in your lives is. You whistle and hiss between your teeth. I have not studied what that might mean, but I think it does have meaning.

You turn. You. . . .

I cannot even think such a thing. I refuse to think it, but!

You pick me up! One hand under where I sit and one hand under my heavy head. My legs dangle. My arms dangle. I would let my long fingers curl around your throat, and don't think it would be the first time I've done it to your kind. We may be weak, but our hands are strong. They were made for just this purpose. They were used from the start for leaping into wombs and from the start for strangling an unruly or a panicked mount, but you hold me low as if you know that.

You don't even take my pole. You don't even tie me up. You put me on a patch of scratchy sand.

The others of you talk, but you do not. There is something wrong with you. If I'd known that, I would never have asked you to speak. I would have been kind. That is our way.

"Kindness is our way," I say.

You all three move from me, to another knob, and sit, knees almost touching. You whisper. Even with my long sharp ears turned towards you, and even with my hands cupped around them to gather yet more sound, I can't hear what you're saying. I say a few Hos. None of you pay attention. Though I have cared so much for you, even you don't care.

I droop. I let my ears dangle against my cheeks. I look down at my whites. They're dirty all over and your sweat has dulled them. I have to study to find a pure spot with any glow to it. What you all must think of me, crumpled here and no glow?

It's time for a meal. Could it ever come to pass that I would have to eat *your* dried treats for my dinner?

But. . . .

Are they leaving? The Sam and Sue and my Sam, too? This is preposterous. It is not to be contemplated. Not to be experienced.

I call a *real* ho. *HO!* with all the overtones I can muster. I feel it rattle in my cheek bones, trumpet in my nose. I stand up. I call out everything I can think about to call.

"You can't leave me out here helpless. I'm a pregnant female, or what you might call female . . . or might call pregnant. What will become of my little ones? They even have their names. I had thought we would have a future together, where my young would play on your shoulders.

"And what about all the things I wanted to tell? Teach? Wisdom and lore? My head is full of what you need to know. Come back. My heart is with your heart. It always is. You may speak. Tell me what you want."

My Sam, my faithful steady—he doesn't even look back.

But I can set your forest blazing, which is your forest, not ours. Except I couldn't flee my own fire. My little wobbly legs . . . must they carry my heavy head? I might go a pace or two.

"Help me. I will show you the secrets of my pole. It isn't much of a secret once you know it. Even you will understand.

"What I want to tell you has to do with the meaning of life. And most especially with the meaning of *your* life—all of you together and *you* in particular.

"I said so before. The meaning of life and of butterflies. Yes, yes, I did say it. Though perhaps not out loud. And the knowledge of time. Which few of you have because it goes on and on into a far future you cannot conceive of and begins in a year which is already ten thousand years old. But I will tell you, and only once, and then you will know it. We will ride in the forest together, backing-and-forthing. That was not the last time.

"Not the last time," I say. "Not! It was not!"

Chapter Two

THE PRINCIPLES OF HUMAN CONFORMATION. Which is the science of us. They have lots of information on that. We know all about ourselves, too, though maybe not as much as they do.

I have a good conformation. They said so when they came to take a look at me and watch me on the go-round. They said I have a nice trot. That didn't just happen. I watched my own shadow while they were watching me, and I tried to keep my head level like they teach us, so no bouncing. Even I can see I have a nice trot.

There were four of us on the go-round, us three Sams and one Sue. I'd never seen them before. I don't get to see many others of my own kind. The Hoots sat on platforms so they could get a good view of us.

Mostly they kept looking at me. "Those legs will develop," they said, and the littlest of them said, "I want that one," pointing at me. When they came down to have a closer look, they said, "Nice teeth, too. At least his diet hasn't ruined them—or his conformation. I'd say he's about eleven." But all of them wish I didn't have such a long nose. If I'm good for showing, they'll have to have it fixed.

They took my picture from all angles. They made me be naked. (They stare too much and they have big round eyes that pop out. That's how they see so much more than we do, front and back at the same time.) Afterwards, I got pats and strawberry ice cream.

They sent the pictures and my fingerprints away for approval and registration. They didn't come to get me till they knew I was guaranteed!

I'm a Seattle. We're the best for size and strength, though we're not as fast as the Tennessees. I want to be a good Seattle. I want to be the best there is.

Back at the old place over my stall, it said, SMILEY, and under that, OUT OF MERRY MARY. *Will make a strong puller, long-distance trotter, and a good stud.* They wrote it in our writing and in theirs. I can read them both.

I'll be free to stand for any Seattle girls. I might even get my choice.

I didn't call my dam Merry Mary. I called her mom. I wish they'd brought her along, though I know I'm too old for having my mother with me. She knew things would be a lot better for me here, but she didn't like to see me leave even so. She wouldn't let go of me until they took a pole to her. I'll bet she has a scar. If I ever see an old Sue with a scar across her face, I'll know it's my mom.

My father's picture is in my registration booklet along with mom's. He was the Sam, Beauty, out of the Sue, Susie Q II Too. Tutu for short. She was a famous endurance racer. There's nobody hasn't heard of Tutu.

I'd like to meet my father someday. I wonder if he still looks like his picture? (I wonder if my nose will get long, too. It's a little bit long already.) At least up to the time of that picture they hadn't had his fixed. I hope they don't do that. How will I know him without his nose? His hair is black and shiny and combed nice and neat for the picture. He's almost naked so as to show his conformation. I wonder what he usually wears? Probably, since he's special, something shiny.

I look at his picture a lot. I wonder if I'll ever get to meet him. He's kind of ugly, but at least he looks different from most Sams, even Seattles. I might know him even if they fix his nose.

First I got here, I tried not doing anything, not getting up and not going out to the gym and the arena. I wasn't sick or tired, I just didn't want to do it, and I wondered what would happen. There's some books here I never saw before. One is about a war that was us against us. I could hardly believe in it, but there were real pictures. There's another about all sorts of animals. I wanted to lie here and read.

I learned, pretty quick, not to ever, ever, ever do that again. And after the poling, I got a kindly talking-to with lots of pats. They took me up over the arena, up where *they* usually sit, and one of them told me how even they have to work all the time, a lot harder than we ever do, and how they get up earlier (they have to feed us, don't they?), before any of them eats. And don't I want to be a good, hard-working Seattle? They depend on me. So now I hitch myself to the go-round all by myself. Now none of them has to wake me up in the morning or corner me to catch me. (That used to be one of my games. It was fun.)

They keep saying *we're* the *really* free ones. They keep saying, "Where would we be without you faithful, sure-footed steadys?" And then they flap their ears (which is their laugh) because they're so happy about having us. It's easy to see, where *would* they be? In their houses they have to scoot around on little stools. I wouldn't like that at all. We really *are* the lucky ones.

Sometimes my new Little Master loves me so much he licks me all over my cheeks and ears. Nibbles, too. The big one tells him, "We don't do that." But my little one does it anyway.

They train us, me and my little one, at the same time. "Tight but light," the big one says to him. "Remember your hand strength."

Our trainer sits on a high stool and watches. He carries a pole long enough to reach the whole round pen. Then he starts to yell—at my Little Master, even though he's His Excellent Excellency About-To-Be-The-Ruler-Of-Us-All.

"Look! Look! Remember every Sam can tell which way to turn by your own head movements. Poke him! Poke! Poke! Far side! If you got poked in one side, which way would *you* move? Give him a pat. He's done well. But never pat for no good reason."

I get tired of hearing the exact same thing every day, but my Little Master has to learn. They yell at him a lot more than they yell at me. They always say if the rider is good then the mount is good.

My Little Master, The-Future-Ruler-Of-Us-All, His Excellent Excellency, is still too young to be masterful. He's so young and little he doesn't understand big words, and he can't say much more than, "Go, go, go," and, "Bad boy. Good boy."

He almost falls off lots of times and sometimes does. He's so awkward, pulls on me and pricks me. Young as he is, they let him wear needles. "Don't you realize how that hurts?" our trainer says. Then he pricks His Excellent Excellency really hard with his own needles. (They don't cry like we do, they just droop their ears and tails.)

Sometimes The-Future-Master pulls my head around hard and leans the wrong way by mistake and makes me fall, too. I'm supposed to not fall, no matter that it's his fault. When I fall, I get a poling.

"See what you made me do?" our trainer says. To me. "Now you'll have another scar. We'll have to paint over that when we show you."

But every now and then we, His Excellent Excellency and I, get a playtime together. We play guess where and guess again where, and I run up and down and lean low so he can see where a thing might be. I hear his ears flap right next to mine. That's his giggle. Sometimes I do a kind of lope that bounces him. Sometimes I twist us around until we're both dizzy. He flaps and flaps. Then we get to sit on the grassy bank and rest together and he pats me. I'm not allowed to pat him back or I would. Except they prefer strokes. It's us primates that pat and like pats.

I don't want to hurt His Excellent Excellency, Future-Ruler-Of-Us-All. I would save him from harm. I keep wondering how I can prove that to them. I'm so tired at quit-time I don't read much anymore. What I do is daydream about how I might find a way to rescue him some day to prove to them how I feel.

Even though my mom isn't here, there's nice things about this new place. We're out in the country—because of fresh, clean air for The-Future-Ruler-Of-Us-All, and they say it's just as much for me. I need good clean air, too. The mount of The-Future-Ruler-Of-Us-All is just as important as The-Future-Master himself.

I can see the mountains and the forest from my paddock. Some pretty close. I wonder if they'll ever let us go there. Excellent Excellency would like it, too. I don't dare ask them, but at playtime I dare ask him if he wants to go and he says, "Oh yes, go, go, go," and flaps his ears like anything.

"We'll go," I say.

"There!" he says, and points with his fingers all spread out as if to grab hold of the forest. I pretend to bite them and then he pretends to choke me.

Then I say, "Guess what?"

"What?"

"My real person name is Charley. Isn't that funny? And guess what? We call all of you Hoots. I suppose because of that big ho you do, so I'm a Sam and you're a Hoot."

He flaps his ears and gives a ho, which we can't begin to imitate even when we try but that their babies can do from when they're first born. He's so close I have to hold my ears until it's over.

I didn't think they bothered listening to us at playtime. And we didn't mean anything real, but they take a pole to both of us. We look at each other because neither of us knows what it's about. Is it because I called him a Hoot and he let me? Or because I said we'd go to the forest and he wanted to, which how could we without a grownup of one of them with us? Or is it because he's not supposed to give a ho unless there's a good reason for it and it's half my fault that he did it?

They usually tell us what's wrong and give us a long talking-to, but this time they don't. After our poling, his Excellent Excellency and I sit beside the round pen and hold hands. Hoots always like to hold hands, especially the little ones. I have tears and he's all droopy, but we don't dare ask anything.

After that we get a couple of rest days, but I don't know why the rest *or* the poling.

I'm living in a big paddock now with a Seattle female. Her name is Sunrise. She's too old to do much but cook for me. She doesn't wear shorts, she wears longs. I guess nobody cares what her legs look like anymore. We have a kitchen and we each have a stall of our own and there's a sitting place out in front with a rocking chair. No walls. We're kept in by just one little white wire. That's all it takes. The Hoots can hear, or maybe feel, if it's turned on or not, but we can't.

The white wire is turned off exactly long enough for me to

hurry back to my paddock if I trot. They like everything done fast. They say there's only so much time and then we die, so do we want to waste it? But I'd like to know what's so important about hurrying back to your paddock?

When I first came, I thought to try and jump it to see what would happen, but then I thought, maybe later when I really want to go someplace. I already had had enough trouble with staying in bed and not doing anything that other time.

These are my first rest days since I got here. I sit out front in our rocking chair and watch the others of us work on themselves. I grew up in a Seattle center, so I haven't seen much but Seattles before, but here there are other kinds of us. I sit and watch those thin ones practice on their speeds. They're *so* odd. I don't like the looks of any of them. They're the sprinters, so they can't be bad if they can go fast. But I'm better than fast. What good is fast when you can't carry heavy loads?

I'm glad I'll never have to be mated with any so thin and with little stick legs. But they wouldn't let me even if I wanted to. Those are the Tennessees. The very shortest distance runners are the Candy/Rex Tennessees. The best of them all come from that single Sam and Sue combination.

I rest and watch and that old Sue, Sunrise, brings me oranges and milk and oatmeal cakes. I get all I want of anything she has in our kitchen. I'm supposed to grow. She's stooped over now, but she used to be bigger. I'm not only taller than she is now, but she says I'm already taller than she used to be.

Mostly she calls me Smiley, but when she comforts me after a poling—like now—she calls me Charley. (Sunrise's person name is Margaret. But I kind of like Sunrise. She's the one who's always smiling. And she hugs a lot and gives lots of pats.) She teaches me things, too. Secrets. She taught me the whistle for *danger*, and for *be quiet* and *hold still*, another for *run*, and another for *hide*. She thought it was important that I know those, but she says I'm too young for any other secrets. Maybe I am, because look how I told things to His Excellent Excellency, except I won't ever do that again, even to him.

I know tunes of old songs mean things, too, though I mostly don't know what. They never say the words that go with the tunes. All they have to do is whistle the first few bars, never the whole thing, and every grownup knows. Love songs are secret, too, because we're not supposed to be in love.

After our couple of days' rest, my Little Master and I go back to practice and everything is like it always is. Then one day I trot into my paddock and I hear whistling that's not the same as the usual. Somebody several paddocks away is whistling like anything—a tune I never heard before. It's not *danger* or *hide* or *run* or anything I know about, and it doesn't seem like one tune, but a lot of them stuck together.

Sunrise says, "That's Molly." So it's a Sue, not a Sam. Then, for a minute, maybe longer, our white wire turns blue and spits sparks all over our front porch. They hurt. Sunrise grabs me and puts her body between the sparks and me just as if she was my own real mom and as if I wasn't taller than she is.

"They're warning us," Sunrise says, still hugging me.

I say, "I hope my little Excellent Excellency is all right."

Sunrise lets go of me. "*Yours!*" she says, then she says, "I guarantee there are no sparks on His Excellent Excellency, The-Future-Ruler-Of-Us-All." She says his whole title, but I can tell it's not out of respect.

I say, "Good," and go into my stall. I wish there was a door to it.

Next evening Sunrise is the one who whistles. Then the sparks come again and I know she made them happen. She shouldn't have done that. I should have stopped her.

Then, at the end of the day, right after she serves me my evening meal, Hoots come. Three of them on big Seattles like us. Those Seattles have different tack. Bits in their mouths and cheek-pieces that have spikes. Their shoes are peculiar and make them seem taller than they already are.

Then Sunrise gets poled. I didn't think they'd do it to somebody so old. They always say how they take such good care of us even after we're too old to work anymore. I try to get in front so the poling will be on me instead, but one of the Hoots poles me away. He's riding the biggest Seattle I ever saw. I look up into the Seattle's blue, blue eyes, but I don't know what I see there. He looks crazy. At first I think sparks will fly out as if his eyes were the white wires. There's hate in him, nothing but, but I can't tell if it's for me or who?

Then a Hoot puts handcuffs on Sunrise and forces a bit into her mouth (first she fights it, but then it looks as if it hurts more to resist than to take it) and one of them gets on her shoulders and rides her away. I want to hug her and hang onto her like my mother did to me, but the big Seattle and that Hoot riding him keep me back. I keep yelling, "Sunrise," over and over. (I wouldn't call her Margaret in front of Hoots. Nobody ever said not to, but I wouldn't anyway.)

I fall to my knees the minute they're gone—the minute that crazy Sam and his Hoot let me go. They're the last to leave. I put my head down on the cement floor. I don't cry. But then I hear whistling not far away. It's "Rock-a-Bye Baby." And after that, "Yankee Doodle Dandy." I do know the beginnings of those songs, I don't know exactly what they mean, but I know they're telling me that even though I'm alone, I'm not alone. Their whistling makes me cry—for Sunrise and for my real mom, too. If Sunrise is gone for good, there's nobody who cares about me. Except His Excellent Excellency. I know he does. Otherwise my whole life all day long is getting yelled at. His is, too.

I finally get up and get into bed. I don't go get my evening snack, I just collapse there and have bad dreams where scraps of everything that happened happen over and over.

The next morning an even older Seattle comes in to look after me. She doesn't talk at all. I don't think she can, because she writes out her name for me, Bonnie Blue Bonnet. Her white hair is yellowish. She has to have a cane even here in our paddock. I know nothing is her fault, but I hate her anyway.

When I go out for practice, I feel like telling my Little Master everything that happened, but I know he can't do anything about it, and I know he might not understand. Well, he *would* understand—he's the only one who would—but they might hear.

It's nice to have his lick, though. It makes my tears come. He licks all the more (he must like the taste) and he gives me lots of pats even though our trainer says, "Stop it," about a dozen times and threatens with his pole. His Excellent Excellency licks my tears off so fast I don't think our trainer notices them. Does my Little Master know about tears? I'll bet he does. He knows lots of things automatically.

So tears come and go, off and on, almost all day as we practice. Afterwards, I feel all cried-out. It's good I do, because I won't cry in front of Bonnie Blue Bonnet no matter how much I feel like it. And I will never, ever call her by name. By any name.

Her cooking isn't as good as Sunrise's anyway. I knew it wouldn't be just by looking at her. It doesn't matter, because I can't imagine ever being hungry again. I wonder how long she has to be here? I'd rather be alone and just eat dry cakes. They're supposed to have everything you need. At that old place that was mostly what we ate all the time.

I let Bonnie Blue Bonnet have the rocking chair. I go in my stall (again I wish I had a door). I think about that Sam's eyes—the way he looked at me so scary. Then I think about Sunrise. I wonder what they do with old Sues when they take them away like that? Then I think about my Little Master. I know where he lives, because it's a special big house with a golden flag on top. You can see it from the arena fence. His Excellent Excellency is proud of it. He points and says, "Mine." If it were mine, I'd be proud of it, too. What if I crossed the white wire now, and, *if* I wasn't too stung by it, what if I went to my Little Master's house? What if I told him about

Sunrise? Except he's not the master of anybody right now, hardly even of me.

Then I stop thinking and listen. It's *so* quiet. I've never heard it so quiet before. What does *that* mean! Then I think how I'm not sure I remember the whistles for anything. I can't ask Bonnie Blue Bonnet. She can't talk and I'll bet she can't even whistle. Her mouth is too puckered up already.

Then I hear a signal. I'm sure it is one, but it's one of the ones Sunrise didn't think I was old enough to know about.

I wait. I don't move. But nothing happens. I keep on waiting, but I'm so tired from crying all day . . . well, I wasn't really crying, just those tears kept coming down . . . and I was thinking so hard and then waiting . . . . I fall asleep without meaning to.

Suddenly yelling and yelling. I jump up and look out. They come. Out from the forest. Down from the mountains. Yelling. Hordes and hordes and hordes! Savages. But us. . . . *Us!* They're killing and killing. . . . Really killing, dragging Hoots out of their houses, beating on them. Even the Tame ones of us that live here are joining with the bad Wild ones. Everybody's jumping over the wires and nothing's happening to them. The sparks are turned off. Bonnie Blue Bonnet grabs my hand and tries to make me jump, too, but I don't want to be like all the others.

Everything is confused, big clouds of dust fly up—into the moonlight. Some of my kind have poles. That's not allowed.

Bonnie Blue Bonnet lets go of me and jumps the wire by herself—if you call that jumping. And then I do, too. I know what to do. It's what I've wanted ever since I got here.

We're not allowed in the Hoots' houses, but now I run to the big one with the gold flag. There's two Hoots sprawled right outside the doorway. I hope they're not dead. If they are, then I've seen my first close-up dead thing. But I don't have time to think about it. The door is so low I have to stoop, and stoop all the way down the hall. I'm like a giant . . . like a clumsy savage . . . like those others of us from the forest. And I feel even more so when I get to the first big room and look around. I have to stop. I never saw anything like it.

They believe in having beauty around them. That's one reason they like us so much, we're so beautiful, our muscles and all. And here, everything is of us, lamps made out of our shoes (brand-new ones, black and shiny), brand-new surcingles with silver on them dangling from the ceiling to hold up paintings . . . of us . . . all of them, of us! Groups of us in the arena or out on the long-distance trails with the forest as our background. In silver frames! I start across the room to look for Little Master, but I have to stop again because I see a portrait that I think might be my father. At least, it's a long face and long nose. I go close and I'm right. Under it there's a silver plaque that says BEAUTY. A little farther along there's my mother, MERRY MARY. After that, there's my picture. Even mine! SMILEY under it. They care about us so much! How can my kind turn against them!

I go on, to the far end of the house. (In these larger rooms I don't have to stoop over.) I look in all the cubby-holes along the walls and finally find my Little Master, all alone in his crib. He has a soft doll of one of us, black-haired like me, in fact just like me. He's hugging it, but when he sees me he lets it go and stands up in his crib—all wobbly like they always are—and reaches up for me to take him as if it was the most natural thing in the world, and I do.

We're not allowed to touch them, especially not His Excellent Excellency, Future-Ruler-Of-Us-All, but I pick him up and help him get around my shoulders. I'm not wearing a surcingle, so it's harder. He hangs on so tight I'm afraid I'll choke. I speak to him though that's not allowed except at playtime. I can hardly get the words out. "Can't. Can't breathe." And he stops and hangs on, just as tightly, but to my hair. I hunker down and crawl us outside. The Hoots have begun ho-hoing all at the same time. So loud it's as if ringing inside my head. I can't think with that going on. My kind is still beating on his kind. I wonder if those Sams and Sues have plugs in their ears.

I leap us away from the sound and the dust and all the banging and bumping of us on them. I don't think about good form or that my hairdo is a mess or that I shouldn't bounce my Little Master, I just get us away, past the fields and into the trees. At first it's hard because so many of us are coming . . . coming and coming in the other direction. I fall a couple of times, but I do it as I've been taught, leaning into my arms and shoulders so as to keep His Excellent Excellency from getting hurt. I keep going until we can't hear any yelling anymore, though I can still hear the ho-hoing, but not as if right inside my head. I've never before trotted so hard and so far at one time, nor over such rough ground. It's good there's a big moon so we can see pretty well.

We stop by a river (partly because I need to rest and partly because I don't know how deep it is. I might drown my Little Master). I help him dismount. He's shaking. He's wet himself and me all down my back. We rest until I can catch my breath. I'm supposed to walk around like they taught me, so as to cool down from so much running. You're not supposed to ever just stop. But I don't. After resting, I stand Little Master on the bank and clean us both up. I can't do much about his whites, but it's better if they don't shine. When we're all cleaned up, I find a resting spot, hidden by bushy trees, and we cuddle in together.

So I've saved him just as I hoped, but I wonder if there's any of them left to know about it?

How could *we! Us!* . . . I'm ashamed to be a Sam. They'll bring disaster on themselves, not on the Hoots. Disaster, like the Hoots have always told us and told us. There's nothing we could ever do to hurt them. They're smarter than we are, they grow the food, and they have all the tools and weapons. They always say to make peace with the way things are. How live without rules the same for everybody? How live without helping each other? They always say it takes strength of character to do your duty under difficult circumstances. They say the work of the world is never done, and they mean themselves, too. Would we like to lie in bed all day? It's not only "Go, go, go," it's "Do!"

Finally it's dawn. Little Master and I come out and look around. This is the first either of us has seen the forest up close in daylight. We sit on a knob and look. Excellent Excellency's eyes seem even bigger than usual. I suppose mine are that way, too. Mostly the ground is a mess, leaves and bark and sticks all over. Nobody's been raking. There are little blue flowers, lots. Yellow ones, too. Lots. We've been stepping on them. Trees, as if out of picture books, bushes that scratched my legs as I ran last night, roots that tripped me. And here, the river. It looks scary.

"Look," the Little Excellent Excellency says. He's pointing here and there and there. "Look, look." Does he know what was happening back home? I guess he does, because he was shaking so and wet us both, but now he's too surprised to think about it.

He reaches to hold my hand with his big one. And then gives it a sloppy lick. (Odd how their hands are so much bigger and stronger than ours while everything else about them is weaker.)

"I love you," he says. "I love you more than our trainer. I only love him a little tiny bit."

He always talks better when he talks to me. I think the others scare him. They're always yelling at him.

Then, "You may speak," he says. As if he's suddenly turned into our trainer himself. Even the same tone of voice.

I don't. Partly because he told me I could. It doesn't seem right for him to say that after I saved him. Besides, he's just a baby.

But I do like him holding my hand and I know he needs to. There's a lot going on with Hoots and their hands that we don't understand. We like to hold hands, too, but I don't think it's the same.

We sit a long time just looking. Pretty soon I wonder if my Little Master is hungry, but I don't ask him. I don't want him thinking about it if he is. I wonder what they eat? I know they don't like ice cream. They don't like cold things even when it's a hot day.

I hear rustling in the forest. I think wild animals. I wasn't scared before, except of the river, but now I move us back under our bushes and we look out. Little Master's ears prick up, one towards the back and one towards the front. Little Master sees them first, of course. It's some of us going by— back into the mountains. Carrying things. Poles mostly, but silver surcingles, old books (they used to be ours, anyway), new shoes. . . . Every Sam or Sue that I get a good look at has a Hoot rain hat. This is all wrong. Those of us up here in the forest are savages. All the Hoots say that, and this stealing proves it.

I should get His Excellent Excellency to a safer place, but I don't think we should go back to our home. At least not yet. Those Sams and Sues don't look as if they'd pay attention to us. They're too busy stealing things. Besides, I may not be full-grown, but I'm a big Seattle—already big as most Sues or any Tennessee. I can defend him against them.

"Let's go," I say, "Let's get out of here."

He says, "I'm scared."

"I won't let anything happen to you. I promise."

"You're not a grownup."

"Besides, we have to find something to eat." I know there isn't anything, but I say that to make him come. "Anyway, let's go see more things. I'm a Sam, too, remember? These Sams and Sues won't hurt me."

"I'm scared anyway. I want my doll."

"Later."

I help him mount. After, I lean over so he can pick some flowers to put behind his ears and mine, too. That makes him feel better. And then we go . . . up along the river. I don't dare cross it.

Every now and then we hear Sues and Sams rustling and whistling signals not far from us. Once in a while there's a part of a song. I wish Sunrise had taught me more, but she didn't think I'd need to know these things so soon. Whenever they're close, I squat down behind something. I don't have to tell him to keep still, he just knows. I can tell how scared he is by how hard he holds on. I depend on him. I wish I could hear things and smell things and see the way he does. But we make a good team just like the Hoots always say, us the legs and them the senses.

One time we hunker down and then we see there's this wild animal with big branching horns. I know from books that it's a deer, but the books didn't say if it's something that would eat us or not. I wonder which one of us is more edible. Little Master is all head. If they like to eat brains, he'd be first. Or maybe they'd save the best for last like I always do.

Anyway, I make a sound by mistake and the deer thing runs away.

We see lots of berries and Little Master wants to eat them, but I know some are poison. Back there we had berries lots of times, but none of these look like any of those. But we're going to have to eat something one of these days. They say those Wild Sams and Sues live on roots. I wouldn't like that.

I'm not trotting as fast as I did. I'm getting tired and it's all up hill, steeper and steeper. Everything's changing. It's getting so there aren't any more bushes for hiding but more rocks for it. When it starts getting dark, we find a place where there's a batch of boulders. We go to hide there for the night, but we see a big long snake crawl out rattling. Back when they warned you about the Hoots' hands, and poison berries, they also warned about rattlesnakes, so we go on. The farther up it gets, the more it's just rocks. Since my kind can't see in the dark, pretty soon we could just lie down in the open and none of those Wild ones would see us, but I go on and on. It's as if I'm so tired I can't think to stop. When I realize that, I sit down right then. "I have to wait till morning. I can't see anymore and I can't think."

"*I* can see," he says.

"*I* know that."

And then he says it. "I'm hungry."

I don't know what to do. I tell him, "In the morning, we'll find something."

We cuddle up together right where we are, middle of nowhere. I think I won't be able to sleep on these rocks and with Little Master on my chest, but I fall asleep before I even know it.

I wake up with Little Master holding me—my ear and my hair—too tight again. At least he's not holding me around my neck this time. It's dawn. I know something's wrong, but I don't know what. I can't hear anything. And then I do. Things coming, lots of them. Do rattlesnakes do that? Come in a bunch to eat you?

But it's us. A minute later we're surrounded—and there's not a single one of his kind riding even *one* of my kind, and not a single one of his kind around to supervise. I've never seen that before.

One of us is just about the biggest Seattle I ever saw. And he's like that one with crazy eyes. Best to run. Maybe he's too big to keep up. But there's Tennessees there, too. I couldn't out-run them.

The big one pulls His Excellent Excellency away from me. That's not easy with both of us hanging on, but he does it, finally, with a jerk. He puts Little Master down on a big stone. Little Master gives one big Ho! like they do when in danger. It's like he can't help it—as if he hardly knew he was going to do that. It echoes all over. Everybody puts their hands over their ears. Except that big one. He raises his pole with both hands and points it at Little Master. He's got crazy, starey eyes, exactly like that other big one that held me away from Sunrise. With eyes like that, you don't know what he'll do. He's got scars on his cheeks, too. And a long, lumpy face and a long nose, and he's nothing but a big bunch of bulging muscles.

I see all this in half a second, and then I jump and get between the pole and Little Master.

It hurts so much I have to sit down and catch my breath. Even though I haven't eaten anything, I feel like throwing up. Nobody moves—none of them, but pretty soon Little Master comes to hug me. I'll have a scar all across me now, forever, top-to-bottom.

When I can breathe again, the big one squats beside me and

looks close into my face. So close I can see the scars all over him. I can see how he needs a shave but there's no hair where there's scars. I can see the brand along his upper lip. He's, even so, a Tame.

"Charley?" He sputters it. Chokes on it.

I say, "That's not fair. He's just a baby." Then, "I thought there was peace."

"Charley? Is it? It's you!"

"My name is Smiley."

"Out of Merry Mary!" There's something wrong with his talking. He can't get the words out. "You're the mount. . . ." He takes a big breath. "Of His Ex. . . ."

The Sue Tennessee finishes for him. "His Excellency, Future-Master. . . ."

But he waves her to stop and goes on by himself. "You *are* Charley. I'm your. . . ." Big breath. "Father."

I see his long nose and long face, and as if my own dark eyes looking back at me. I know he's right. It's Beauty! I knew it even before.

"You're not my father."

"Look at me. Look . . . how alike. The raid . . . partly . . . partly I wanted to rescue . . . and you rescued yourself."

Rescue!

I hate him.

They have a cream my father puts on my top-to-bottom burns. Down my neck and shoulder and ribs and hip bone, down my thigh, and even across my foot. My father puts it on as gently as Sunrise used to put the same kind of stuff on me after I got poled before, but I never got poled this hard. That would have killed my Little Master.

They let Little Master stay next to me. He licks my cheeks and pats me all through it. It's a bother, but I don't tell him.

Afterwards, our stomachs growl as if they were talking to each other.

"You're hungry," that Sue Tennessee says.

I never was this close to one. I never wanted to be and I still don't, she's *so* ugly—she's got little spots all over her—but she's trying to be nice.

Little Master says, "Yes," but I say, "No." And then Little Master says, "Yes, he's hungry, too."

Everybody sits down with the rocks for chairs and tables. My father sits on the ground at my feet. I hate him, but I can't help thinking how he has a *very* good conformation. I can't help thinking how I'll grow up to be as strong as he is.

I never saw some of this food. I don't know what it is, which I guess is a good thing. It doesn't taste too bad, though, and they do have our kind of dry cakes. I'll bet they stole them from the Hoots when they were down there stealing things. Little Master only eats the dry cakes. He knows those because he used to chew on mine even though they told him not to.

After we eat I learn how strong my father is. First he puts the Little Master on my shoulders. He makes him keep one leg off my poled shoulder, so he's sideways. I'm thinking, even sideways, I hurt too much to carry him anywhere, especially not up. But then my father lifts me, easy as could be, and puts both of us on his own shoulders. I'm almost twelve and big for my age, even as a Seattle, but he starts out, straight up the mountain, as if we were nothing. It's a hard climb, but my father hardly even breathes heavily and doesn't stop to rest. I'll be just as good someday. My Little Master, grownup by then, too. We'll go everywhere together, just like we were born for.

We go up all morning, until we finally top a rise, and then start down again. We go around a rocky cliff and there's suddenly a big view of a valley with streams that shine in the setting sun, and green squares and yellow squares and funny houses. Snowy mountains in the background.

Hard to tell from here, but there's nothing there that looks like stalls or arenas, and not a single house looks like the round white lumps, all in a row, that are the Hoots' houses. Not even one. And not a single flag. In fact, hardly any color at all, though when we get closer I can see flowers here and there next to the houses. And, closer, you can see there aren't any white wires. I look hard, but they're not anywhere.

My father points down there. "Margaret . . . your Sunrise," he says. And the Tennessee says, talking for my father, "We rescued her, too. She'll be glad we rescued you. She was worried."

I'm thinking how it was Sunrise's own fault. She shouldn't have been whistling like she did that night, but I say, "Good," anyway, to be polite. Then I ask my father the most important thing. "Are you going to kill him?"

"Not if. . . ."

You can tell it hurts him to talk.

". . . if you don't want. . . ." Big breath. "Want me to."

I guess I don't hate him quite *completely*, but pretty much.

Chapter Three

$By\ now$ I know that rattlesnakes don't eat people. By now I know how to catch and skin and cook them. And I know how to build a fire out of almost nothing, even in the rain. It's my father taught me all the rattlesnake killing and skinning and such. Back down at home I wouldn't have had to know any of that, though with things as they are, it may come in handy.

We went out alone, me and Little Master and my father, and I didn't get to like my father any better. It's not his bigness that scares me. . . . (He leaned close to show me how to hold the firebow, and his arm was the size of about four of mine. Hairy, too, and nothing but wadded-up muscles. I'm glad Hoots don't have any hair except that little bit of red fuzz on the top of their heads.) What scares me is that crazy look in his eyes, how quiet he is, and the way he stares off at the mountains—or at nothing—or at me. That's the scariest. And I wish he wouldn't try to talk.

I'm called Charley all the time now. They only call me Smiley as a joke because I frown so much. I still get to carry my Little Master on my shoulders. No one has dared to stop me, because my father is on my side about this. At least on this one thing.

Even my Little Master mostly calls me Charley now. He still droops sometimes . . . lots of times. He puts his ears down by his cheeks. Not "put"; it's that the Hoots let their muscles go, so nothing holds their ears up. They just flop. I treat him better than his own kind did, but he's sad anyway. He wants his house and his cozy cubby and crib and his kind of food. (Just as much as I want the kind of food I used to have.) And even though he's here with me (he has me closer than he ever had before), he misses his doll, which is a copy of me. We sleep in the same lean-to, so I don't see why I won't do instead, but he says I'm too big to hold easily and I wiggle around in bed too much. We start the night together though—his leg partly around my neck, sort of as if he was still riding me. It's good his legs are skinny and soft.

Margaret/Sunrise made him a new doll, and he was polite about it (Hoots are always kind), but he still wants the old one. It was worn out, but even so, realer than the one she made. It was made of Pliable. We don't have any of that up here, so Margaret had to use cloth. She embroidered my face on it, my hair, of fine black yarn, my eyes, not quite as dark as the hair. I like it a lot, so Little Master gave it to me.

He keeps asking if I'll take him back home to get his old one. I always say yes, but I have to think about how we could sneak away and when. My father wouldn't want me to go. Nobody here would.

I'm feeling pretty droopy myself. They keep telling me I'll

get used to it. They keep telling me it's a lot better to be bosses—all of us masters of ourselves and each other. They say we live free. Well, what we do is, we vote. "Democratically" is what you call it. They say it's a lot better, but if it's so much better, how come we have to get water way down at the creek where we have a barrel-on-a-pulley-sort-of-thing that goes up and down a steep bank? What's so democratic about that? Except that it's the same for everybody. And the water's icy cold. If we want it warm, we have to heat it up ourselves. And light! There isn't any! What little there is comes from candles and fires and oily lamps. You can hardly read without getting so close you could burn yourself up. They have a lot of books, though—in a special book cave. They also have a press so they can make even more. I always did like books—when I had time for them. There's not much more time for them here than there was back home.

I want to go back there just as much as Little Master does. I like our old stalls with hot-and-cold running water and fancy kitchens, heaters you can turn on any time you want. *When* we go, I'll pick up a few things, too. What I want most is that picture of my mother that was framed in silver. Maybe there's some real food left there, too. I'm strong. I could bring back a lot of things, though that picture will be awkward. Little Master and his doll will be on me, too. Maybe I'll only be able to bring that one picture for myself.

They say there's nobody down there in our town anymore, but what if there was? Even one? Somebody that got forgot? One of us, all alone, or one of them, trying to live life rolling around on his little stool? Maybe Little Master and I could stay and help out. Besides, there are too many skinny Tennessees all over the place here, and they walk around as if they thought they were just as important as us Seattles. They're all so set on democratic here, I haven't found anybody I dare ask about what you call the other thing.

The worst is, my father is in love with one of *them*. It's that freckled one who was trying to be nice up when they captured us. They're going to get married. (We don't have marriages there with the Hoots, and the Hoots don't either. I don't see any point in marriages. Little Master says, "Us Hoots always say it makes trouble. Especially for Sues and Sams. They have to breed true. That's for the good of everybody.")

I guess my drooping shows because my father sits me down, exactly like the Hoots always did, to explain things. Except he puts his arm around me. Heavy arm. He never talks much—it's too hard for him—so I wonder all the more what he's going to *try* to say.

We leave Little Master with Margaret/Sunrise. He's safe with her. She's good to every creature. She doesn't care what kind you are. You could even be a rat. Maybe even a rattlesnake. Little Master doesn't like it—he knows she won't host him—but he knows she'll protect him.

My father takes me out to the cliffs above the creek. We can't get close because the banks are too steep. We sit on rocks way up and look down at it. My father has on worn, handmade sandals that have ragged pieces of them hanging out. They're made of some sort of fiber. I suppose I'll have to wear things like that when I outgrow these shoes.

I want to ask a hundred things. Like about the other word for when it's not democracy, and why didn't they find a better place to put their houses than way up here, but I don't because I know he doesn't want to waste any of his talking.

"It takes . . . time," he says, as if everybody hasn't already told me that over and over, including him. Then he kind of coughs and jerks and finally goes on. "This. . . . We're free. When you're older. . . ."

He always stops in the wrong places. That's what makes it so hard to listen.

" . . . be voting."

I say, "I vote for hot water." I look at his sandals. "I vote for shoes."

"Wouldn't you like. . . ." Another stop. "Your own life?" Stop. "Not be ridden? Not told? Where? Forced? Whenever they! *They!*"

I can't stand to try to listen to him. When he taught me how to catch rattlesnakes and marmots, and how to make fires and dig up Solomon Seal, there was hardly any talking at all.

"Wouldn't you rather. . . ." Wait. Cough.

And I can't stand the way some of his scars pull his lips to one side. I can't stand looking at his fuzzy eyebrows.

" . . . with your own people?"

"I *was* with my people. And what about the Tennessees? They're not my people."

He sits looking at those sandals of his. They're ugly, but I'll bet he doesn't care, just so they're made here and by Sams and Sues that vote.

"That's how they want us . . . one against another. . . ." Wait. Jerk. "Charley . . ."

44

It's always even harder for him to say my name. It sticks in his throat.

"I came . . . partly . . . for you."

"My mother," I say, "Why don't you rescue her?"

That stops him. I mean even more than he already is stopped. He cares about that skinny Tennessee, but he doesn't care about my mother at all.

He takes his hand off my shoulder and stays stopped for a while. Then he makes a move as if to put his heavy, sandpapery hand on my arm (hands that have been moving too many rocks), but I flinch away just in time.

"You have . . . *have* to understand. The Hoots. . . . They . . . needed more Seattles. Like me. Like Mary."

"Having me was just a job you had to do. You never even liked her. You don't even like me."

"Charley!" It's like he's choking on my name, but he says it twice more anyway. "Ch . . . Ch . . . Charley."

I say, "I'm Smiley out of Merry Mary. I love her. She has a scar across her face—because of me. She tried to keep me."

He picks stems from the clumps of stiff grass beside us—for no reason I can tell. (There's no real grass anywhere around here and it isn't even green.) He keeps looking down the bank to the noisy, rushing creek, takes a big breath, then more silence, then, "I'll try," he says.

"You will?" If he says he will, I'll bet he really will. "When? How?"

"The runners. Tennessees. The ones who wear . . . cam . . . mouflage. Though no way the Hoots don't see us before. . . . Hear us . . . smell . . . before. It's from runners that I knew

where you were and what they were. . . ." Stop a whole minute.
" . . . making of you. It was selfish of me, but we saved a lot of
others." Another stop. "Got . . . a lot of . . . important. . . ."

"Yes, I know, a lot of hats."

But I feel funny, thinking maybe I could get to see my
mother.

My father stands up. "Come. I'll. . . ."

He doesn't bother finishing. He starts climbing down the
steep bank, and then, when we get to the creek, he starts
climbing on up beside it. It's very rocky. *Big* rocks. Sometimes
you have to step over parts of the stream which, if you stepped
into it by mistake, you'd be swept away. Even my father would.
Even though he looks like a bunch of rocks all stuck together
(feels like it, too), he's not *that* strong.

But why is everything around here so hard to *do!* There's not
a single place smoothed out. Not one. He'll ruin his sandals
even more than they already are. But I suppose his Tennessee
lover will make him more.

Just when I'm beginning to wonder if we'll get someplace
before it's time for supper (and I'm already hungry, I've been
hungry ever since we got up here), we come to where the cliffs
on each side are even steeper than they have been. We start
climbing one side that has little handholds and footholds.
Now and then there's a chain imbedded in the rocks to help
pull ourselves up with. Pretty soon we get to a cave with ruins,
except, once you get far enough in, you see they're fixed up. The
ruined part is out in front, all tumbledown; behind that, everything is nice. Well, as nice as things get up here.

My father doesn't say a single word. And thank goodness.

He leads me all around. He even shows me a big batch of Hoot poles. I don't ask anything because I don't want him to talk. I was surprised he talked as much as he did back there on the bank. (How can you get to know somebody who hardly ever talks and always looks at you with a crazy stare?)

I do see the reason for a place like this . . . for *them* . . . for Wild Sams and Sues hiding out, but, if you lived up here, look how hard it would be to get water! Even worse than where they are now. You'd have to climb all the way down the cliff and then up with the water. And this is supposed to be what free is!

I know . . . I do know my father used to be one of those with spikes at their cheeks and even spikes inside their mouths, and great big-soled shoes like the Sams that hauled Sunrise away. One almost trampled her under his metal soles. Nobody told me but it isn't hard to guess. He's gritting his teeth all the time. He has frown lines as if he's either angry or thinking much too much—except maybe not when he looks at that freckled Tennessee. No, that's not true, he looks angry even then. Her person name is Jane and her Hoot name is Bright Spot. I suppose because of her freckles. My father likes to call her Bright Spot. He takes her hand as if he's the way the Hoots are about holding hands. But he looks angry even when he's happy—if he ever really is happy. Maybe he can't be. But I know he likes it out here in the middle of nowhere. He stares at the mountains as if it's those he loves the most of all. Or maybe hates—it's the same old stare for everything.

That Tennessee comes and puts her arm around him and then she stares, too. They watch the glow from the setting sun turn the mountains pink and purple, and the shadow of the opposite mountains move across the valley, and then they watch the moon come up. Inside the house, I've seen my father stare into the fire that same way, with his writing pad on his lap. I've seen him hardly write but two lines all evening.

He did promise I could keep my Little Master. He's an important man, so when he says something, then that's what has to be. That's not voting. He's not so democratic. Especially not with *me*. I don't get to vote on anything—so far not one single thing, except I can keep Little Master. He tells me what to do all the time—and other people, too. It's not just his size, but his silence, and the way he stares, scares them like it does me. I don't think he hits people. Which is a good thing, because he's the strongest person around. I wonder how many Tennessees it would take to hold him down? I can hardly wait till I get to be like that. *Then* I guess I'll get to vote. I guess I'll have more votes than anybody.

Finally we climb on down—down and down and down and then up, over the bank, and past where we were sitting. Of course we're late for supper. There's nobody left in the dining hall, but they saved us some stew. Who would ever want this mess? But I do now. (If it was rat stew, or even mouse, they wouldn't tell me. Or marmot.) Jane serves us. It's just us three. (My Little Master is still with Sunrise.) Every time Jane puts a plate down or picks one up, she finds a way to linger her hand on my father's shoulder or the back of his neck or his head.

Before he sits down, my father takes his hunting knife and cuts off a dangling weedy string from his sandal, and I think how Little Master and I had better get on down to our town while I still have good shoes that fit me so I can pick up a bigger pair. (What with that Tennessee pawing all over my father, I want to get out of here even faster.)

As we eat, just as silent as usual, I *do* ask my father something I've been wondering. "Is Heron your person name and Beauty your Hoot name or what?"

Jane frowns at me.

"I have no . . . person . . . name." He says it as if he doesn't want one. You'd think, of anybody around here, he'd want one most of all. Then he says, "Beauty later," as if spitting. "Heron . . . was first."

Here we all eat together at a couple of long tables and benches in a long stone house (there isn't much wood). You'd think it would be noisy, but it's quiet except for the children sometimes. I think it's my father, makes everybody quiet. I think when such a big person stares around and never says anything, it makes everybody not want to talk.

The children eat in an alcove at a smaller table. I'd have to eat there, too, because of my age, but, because of my size, I get to eat with the grownups. Also, my father keeps me next to him. Also, I eat with my Little Master beside me. I have to keep him away from the others, especially the young ones of us. It's dangerous for him here and he knows it. Everybody wants to leave him out on the mountain without a mount, too far away to crawl back.

I'm glad I don't have to eat with those young ones. I'm not friends with any of them. On purpose. There isn't a single other Seattle child there. You can tell right away. Small and smaller, thin and thinner. Except one fat girl might be. I've heard the Hoots say that some Seattles have a tendency to fat if they're not worked properly. If she was down there—home—she'd look like she's supposed to look.

Little Master and I live with my father and that Tennessee and Sunrise, and one other Sue and Sam couple. Those two are not Seattles and not Tennessees either. I don't now what they are. They're probably from those random matings the Hoots warn us about. They're nothing. Nobody. I only talk to them if I have to.

We have three small rooms and the lean-to where Little Master and I sleep. That lean-to was stuck on after we came. Even though there's a stone wall between us and the rest of the house, we can hear my father having nightmares. Little Master always comes to hug me when that happens. I'm glad he does.

That Tennessee of my father's tries to talk to me lots of times, but I walk away. Even if she asked if I wanted ice cream I wouldn't answer. (They do have some up here. They go higher for ice.) Anyway, I don't know how to talk to Tennessees. I've hardly said a word to a single one in my whole life so far and I don't think I'll ever want to.

She calls my father "my dear" right in front of everybody. She'd better not try that with me.

These are supposed to be our kind of houses with our kind of things in them, but my kind of house would have hot-and-cold running water and a heater and refrigerator (not an icebox and a fireplace) and a nice, airy bed and the blankets wouldn't be heavy and scratchy. Where I'd put my house it wouldn't be so cold and windy. And in my world everybody would have *real* shoes.

Besides, I just can't get used to seeing all of us Sams and Sues walking around with no Hoots on them. They look like half-people.

I'll be glad to get home. Maybe we won't ever come back. *Everything* down there can't be all smashed up. And there's other towns. Our town wasn't even a big one.

I tell Little Master to be ready to go pretty soon. I hope the rest of us don't notice how his ears are up now and swivel back and forth. He's paying attention and all of a sudden liking everything, even the place, even the food. Makes me wonder why bother going anywhere, just *say* we're going to go. Except I know he'd droop again if it didn't happen. Besides, I want to go as much as he does. I can't wait to get out of here.

I don't tell Sunrise about us going. She's like a mother to me, but I don't anyway. I give her a big hug. She never likes to get hugged when I have Little Master riding me, but she's pleased anyway. She says, "What's that for . . . all of a sudden?"

"Breakfast.

"We should eat more often," and then, "Oatmeal?" and then, "Charley?"

But we're halfway out the door already.

"*Charley!*"

She *is* suspicious. She waves her potholder at us, irritated. "What was that for?" But she won't stop us.

One good thing about this place, we have chores, but nobody

keeps track of us. Not even my father. He did in the beginning, but not anymore. At first he stayed beside me, not only to protect me and Little Master from the others, but to teach me things about living here. Like now we'll not be scared to pick all the mountain currants we want on the way down.

Chapter Four

We're supposed to go help in one of the far fields where my father will be gathering dandelions for supper (dandelions!) but, halfway there, we turn towards the pass. Once we get around the big rock they call the sleeping dinosaur, nobody can see us, and we don't hurry anymore.

(I didn't know about dinosaurs until we got here. The Hoots don't care about them. They care more about us than any things that old and so long gone. Here there's lots of books about them in the library cave. I do like dinosaurs, I don't know why, because it's easy to see how there's no need to bother with them. As the Hoots would say, we mustn't waste time. There's life to be lived and prepared for, not to mention flags to fly and races to be won. And they're right, because why know, when dinosaurs have been dead millions of years? You can't even count back that far if you start right now.)

I trot along and Little Master flaps his ears, giggling and giggling—at birds and marmots and flowers and the whistles of pica . . . at nothing. He sings a Hoot kind of song that I know I can't hear even half of because of my person-type ears. "La la low lee la and love and beautiful, and you, my steady. You . . . and you, sturdy steady, *faithful* sturdy steady, you take me home, and you go, go, go." I never heard him sounding so much like a grownup Hoot, and he's never called me "faithful sturdy steady" before. I like it. It's what I always try to be.

We climb to the pass and across and over. It'll be down all the way from now on, a long, long, all-day down. Maybe two days down. After I tell Little Master that, he sings it: "La, lee, long, long, all day long, long, and long, long going on down."

I feel . . . just like he does. *So* good! I always do when I trot along like this, fast. My father's wrong. We *were* made for exactly this, for carrying hosts—like the Hoots are always saying. Nothing else feels this good: To run and to be helping the helpless go somewhere and being called sturdy and steady and faithful.

I tell Little Master maybe the town is rebuilt by now and full of Hoots. "They'll be glad to see us. I'll be special because I saved *you.*"

Then I yell, "Yes!" Yell and yell it for no reason.

He yells it, too. "Yes! His Excellent Excellency, About-To-Be-The-Ruler-Of-Us-All! *You've* saved me! *Yes!*"

He hasn't said his whole real name for a long time, not since we got up there. Now he shouts it—almost as loud as a Hoot ho. I turn my head away and lean over and hold my ears, but that doesn't help when a Hoot is stuck right to you and hoing.

"You're hurting my ears."

"Sorry."

"It doesn't do any good to whisper *now.*"

Back up there at the Sam and Sue town, nobody cares about The-Future-Ruler-Of-Us-All and his mount. I wasn't even special—except maybe for being so big for my age and for being my father's son. He's to blame for this whole thing. He led everybody down the mountain. They're all proud of themselves. They think they'll be famous. They're putting it in their new history books. I think it's what you call pillaging and plundering. I read about that. Those vandals.

But my father doesn't care anything about those raids except he's glad about getting me. He says he wants to be a farmer and live up even higher. All by himself, except maybe with me and his Jane. I can't think of anything worse. Who does he think I am, anyway? I always liked civilized. I always cared a lot about art, though I didn't get to have or do any.

Is it all right to not like your own father?

The one and only thing I really do like about him is how I'm going to be like a bundle of rocks myself. If you kick me, you'll stub your toe.

We stop and pick mountain currants every time we see a nice patch. Little Master doesn't even dismount. We pick, head to head, cheek to cheek. We like it that way. Sometimes he puts what he picks into my mouth, and sometimes I put what I pick into his. We drop a lot but we don't care. He giggles with his ears, and I giggle with my mouth.

We spend the night in the same spot where we hid that time with everybody climbing back with stolen things. It's where a big tree fell. Its roots are slanted sideways so they make a kind of wall, and there's bushes in front. We still have a long ways to go. I didn't realize how far and fast I'd trotted that night—

a lot farther than I thought I ever could, all at once like that and mostly up. I didn't even stop to rest one single time. Our trainer would have given me lots of pats if he'd known about it. I hope someday he does.

It's this night, as I lean against the big, uprooted roots, that I start to worry about what might be down there. I had been thinking that all I had to do was to get back home and everything would be all right, but what if there's nothing but dead bodies all over the place, and what if everything is squashed, houses and all, even our stalls? Maybe I should leave Little Master in a safe spot at the edge of the forest and go get his Smiley doll and my mother's picture and come right back— not even bother with new shoes and some really good food.

I can't sleep. I just doze a little. In the morning I think to creep away before Little Master wakes up. This is a good spot, and by now I know deer and rattlesnakes won't eat him, but there's mountain lions, though I've never seen one in all this time. And there might be things my father forgot to tell me about or got tired of trying to twist his lips around to say them. I'd better not leave Little Master yet.

I wait until we get down where the forest ends and the fields begin, then I say I'll find him a safe spot, maybe up in a tree, while I go get his doll. "You can sit and sing to yourself," I say. Trouble is, I say it before I squat to let him dismount. He gets a real Hoot grip on me. There's nothing I can do. I don't even bother trying. I've tried before, back when we were in the arena horsing around. Anything that has to do with hands, he always wins. Funny how even their newborn babies have stronger hands than ours. (Those babies are almost nothing but heads and hands—they're *so* cute—and they can't say anything but squeaky hos. Loud, though. The teeny new ones ho so high we can't hear it.)

It's late afternoon. We should probably spend the night where we are, hidden in the trees and bushes at the edge of the fields, but now that we're so close, we're too eager to see what's happening at home. I warn him, "We mustn't get our hopes up."

We step out from the trees into the fields. There's nothing but flowers—red-orange ones—all over. No irrigation anymore, so everything else is dead, and there's these little flowers instead. Little Master yells, "Don't step on them." I try, but there's no way not to. They're everywhere.

I haven't seen these fields except from a distance or that night in the dark. Mostly I just went to and from the arena, past stalls, all painted white, and then the Hoots' houses— bunched together, all white, too, and the Hoots in their shiny whites. All that white made the fields in the distance seem even greener. (Hoots eat mostly green things.)

I don't trot. Trotting down all day is worse than climbing up, and I'm tired, but I walk a nice fast walk. Smooth, like I've been taught.

Those flowers look so nice they give me energy. Little Master, too. He lifts his head from resting it on top of mine, kicks his feet against my chest, and makes happy humming sounds and every now and then a "La, lee, low, and go, go, go."

But the closer we get, the more the town doesn't look right. All of a sudden we're not so happy anymore. And we're scared. I tell Little Master to keep looking around and sniffing and listening. I tell him I depend on him like I always do, but now it's more important than ever.

We walk past squashed Hoot houses. The Sam and Sue stalls aren't quite so bad. They're made of wood and harder to knock over. Those scary white wires still run all along the edges of the paddock porches and front lawns, but Little Master can hear right away that they're turned off and tells me not to worry.

I find our paddock, Sunrise's and mine. I *think* it's ours, but they're pretty much alike, and all our special things are gone. The refrigerator's gone. Little Master can hear that there's no power for it anyway. No stove, no rocking chair, not even any of my books.

"Let's find your house," I say. But that will be hard since they're all so flattened, and we can see even from here that there's no gold flag on top of any of them.

Little Master says he can tell where it is if we go to the arena and start from there. He's rolled to it on his stool after practice. Even all by himself a couple of times. That was one of his tests. "Hoots can smell the way to go," he says. "And we can feel the lines of the earth."

When we find it, it seems even more squashed than the others, as if us Sams and Sues were mad that it had a gold flag. What we'll do is figure out from the outside where his cubby was and dig right over where we think his crib is. After that we'll figure out the hall where my mother's picture is. Those are the important things.

But it's getting dark. We go back to the stalls and find a nice one to curl up in. It has cots but no pads and no blankets. It's not so cold down here anyway. (Another reason why it's dumb for my kind to live way up there and no heaters.)

Little Master and I curl up together like we do. We're both so tired we fall asleep right away, but I don't stay asleep long. I hear funny noises. Little Master is so sure of me looking after him, he sleeps like he always does when I'm close by—as if I'll keep him safe—his leg across my shoulders and breathing long, slow breaths, his baby mouth open and kind of drooly. (They have nice curvy lips when they're little.) But I'm not that sure of myself, and I worry.

Some of those funny noises are like the ones we hear up there in the mountains, mice and such, but I've never heard things like that down here. The Hoots kept all that stuff away. They say even a mouse couldn't cross the white wires. With those wires there, they say we couldn't even have fleas. We had those back where my mother was.

So I don't sleep much this night either. I'm thinking I might even like to go back up there in the cold, with lots of Sams and Sues and my big father in the next room. I don't get back to sleep until dawn, when I start to feel safer. Of course Little Master wakes up just after that, all excited about going to get his doll. I get up. I still mostly do what he says. I *especially* do it now, when we're back home here where I used to always have to.

But I don't feel good. I need a big drink of nice cold water and I need to wash up. Except the faucets don't work, neither hot nor cold. Not in this stall nor in any of the next ones either. Little Master says he can smell that there's no water anywhere near except down at the pond.

We have our first real argument. I should say fight. Dumb because he's still just a juvenile. It's as if I'm arguing with a two-year-old. There's no point. I know better but I do it anyway. I don't feel like being nice to anybody.

When we find out there isn't any water, he says, "Find some. Heat it and wash me. And I'm thirsty."

He hasn't ever acted that way with me before. Doesn't he think I'm as thirsty as he is? I want to yell at him but I don't. I'm slipping back into the silence all us Sams and Sues were taught first thing. I can feel it—how I'll get poled if I speak or even make an unnecessary noise, though we don't even have a pole.

At first I stutter and sputter, but then I'm all right. "You think I'm not thirsty, too? I don't think you Hoots are always so nice to us Sams and Sues like you keep saying you are."

He says, "You're a mess. Go straighten yourself out," exactly like our trainer always said it. He hasn't said that ever in his whole life that I know of. And why does a juvenile care about hair? Besides, there's no shows to be spic-and-span for. (Besides, with my big, long scars, I'm not sure I'll ever be able to be shown, nose fixed or not.) Being down here isn't good for either of us. And since when did a mount have to wash a host, anyway?

(I'm thinking, if we were back up there, we could vote on who would do what, except there would be one vote each. So *that* proves something about voting.)

"My father was badly mistreated. Badly. Disciplined with poles and spikes. I'll bet he was one of those in big boots with prickers at his cheeks, *and* in his mouth. He has scars all over."

"He probably tried to run away. That's a waste of valuable time. He didn't know what was good for him."

I can't believe how he's saying—word for word—what our trainer always said.

"Valuable is a big word for a baby."

"Besides, us Hoots *are* nice. Always peaceful and kind. That's the one sure thing. We *have* to be, it's the only way. We depend on you. We love you. We always give you praise and pats. Now get me water."

Then I see his hands in that position. Every Sam and Sue knows what that means. Their warning is always in their hand positions, out in front and ready to choke something. I move back a little. Hoots may not be able to walk much, but they do have one big leap in them when they're squatting down like that. And of course everything they do is much faster than we can ever do. I was taught all about that by Merry Mary from the start. And back up there in the mountains, when my father taught me about rattlesnakes, I thought of Hoots right away. Rattlesnakes can coil up faster than you can see. (My father stamped near one to show me.) And then they strike before you know it. Hoots do, too. If they get their hands around your neck, you're done for in a couple of seconds because your Adam's apple gets pushed in to where you breathe. Little Master has never made this gesture towards me—except as a joke, in play.

I move three yards away. Considering he can spring out about twice his own length, that should be more than enough room. He'll be sorry. I'm not sure I'll ever want him on my shoulders again. Why would I want a rattlesnake on me?

I say, "You snake!"

"Hush, you know better than to speak."

"After all this time! And all I've done!"

I turn right around and leave. I'll go to find water for myself. I know where it is. We followed a stream most of the way. It goes right down the middle of town, right to the pond with a fountain and the statue of a mounted Hoot in the middle. I've been there two or three times. Of course with Little Master on my back. They never would have let me go anywhere by myself. We had a couple of playtimes there when Little Master got to steer me around wherever he wanted. Our trainer was right behind us. Little Master led me into the pond up to my knees, and we floated toy boats.

The pond's still there but it's been blown up. There's water in it, except it's half the size it used to be and the statue with the mounted Hoot is gone. That makes me sad. Especially since the mount (of course) was a Seattle. The ducks and baby ducks are there. The baby ducks are eating and the mothers are watching over them. First I think about mothers in general, and then I think how Merry Mary watched over me. I'm thirsty, but for a minute my throat is too closed up for me to swallow, let alone drink. If my father doesn't find Merry Mary, then I'll look for her myself. Her face will be scarred and she'll be older, but I'll know her. I'm changed, too. I have my long, life-long scar up and down me, and I'm not wearing what we used to wear. Hoots always liked us Seattles to show off our legs. Now I have leggings to protect from brush and cold. And I have a kind of vest thing that that Tennessee, Jane, knit for me. She knit one for Little Master, too. She keeps trying to get on my good side, just like my father always tries to.

I sit there—wishing things: For my mother, and for the town to be as it was, and for Little Master to be like he was. I used to think how he was the only one who really understood me. Pretty soon tears come because now there isn't anybody.

I don't want to cry. I don't think a Seattle ever should, anyway. My father wouldn't. He's too big.

I take off my shoes and jump in the pond. That shocks me out of crying. The water's ice cold like it is up in the mountains. Well, that's where it comes from. I drink and wash—as best I can without soap. Then I forget for a minute and wonder how to carry water back to Little Master. Or should I bring him over here? I guess I do want to go back and help him, except I'm not sure I want to get close enough to let his hands anywhere near me.

I forgot something when I jumped into the pond. I went in with our biscuits. They're soggy. I lay them out to dry, but I'll have to keep an eye on them or the ducks will steal them.

I put my shoes back on and search around. Partly for something to carry water in and partly just to look around. *I'm* in no hurry. I want Little Master to get good and worried. I check out how hard it's going to be to get into a Hoot's squashed house. The stucco part isn't hard, but there's this mesh under it. You can't cut it, but every now and then there's a seam where you might be able to pull it apart.

Then I see somebody coming. Running. A Sam, and no Hoot on him. (I'm still not used to seeing that. It shocks me, especially here at home.) I trot away from the creek and hide behind some Hoot-house debris.

It's a Tennessee. One of those runners, dressed in camouflage. First he dips his whole head in the pond. Then drinks and spits, then fills his canteen and leans to drink again. I hate how those Tennessees look . . . all stringy . . . all bones.

He looks like he's been running a long ways, so I guess they can run as far as we can, but I don't like his looks anyway. For sure they can't carry much, not like my father carrying me *and* Little Master up—*steeply* up the mountain.

I'd like to ask this one where he comes from and where he's going, but I can't make myself. He's too much like that one my father's going to marry. I might be able to talk to her if she wasn't going to marry my father, but I don't see how he can stoop to that. They won't have any children like me. They'll all be freckled pipsqueaks. Maybe that's why my father likes me— enough to come all the way down here to get me.

But what if I ask this runner about my mother? What if he knows where I could find out something about her? If he has paper, I could write her a note. The Hoots never let us do that, they thought it would be bad for us, but nobody would stop me now.

The Tennessee stands up and looks all around. He sees my drying dry cakes and looks all around again. Then he takes a big, blowy breath. He's going to run again, but it's easy to see he doesn't want to.

If I'm going to ask him anything, I'd better do it now.

I sneak out from behind the broken bits of Hoot house as quietly as I can. But he's not a Hoot, I don't have to be *that* careful. And any Hoot would have smelled me and heard me a long time ago.

I suppose I should have stepped out right away, made a noise, not come at him from behind, but I don't know much about us Sams and Sues. I've only known a few really well. I was always in a stall with only one other person. And I worried what that Tennessee might think when he sees my scars. (It's been months and they still hurt.) Only really bad Sams get scars all up and down themselves like mine. (And only really, *really* bad Sams are scarred up like my father.)

The Tennessee startles and turns and jumps at me—he seems as fast as a Hoot. He has a long knife. I almost get another scar.

You can tell he knows what he's doing . . . I mean, how to fight, which I don't. He holds the knife low and upside-down. I want to learn that. I'll bet my father knows. I wonder why he didn't show me?

Being a Seattle, even though I'm only eleven, I'm taller than he is, but I think he sees I'm a young one and holds back just in time.

"Sorry. *Maybe* sorry." He looks at me, my scars and how I'm all wet. "Which side are you on?" He's staring at me almost as hard as my father does. "You for refrigerators and nice warm stalls, or what? There's lots of Sams haven't decided where the strawberry ice cream comes from."

I can't answer. I don't know which side I'm on. All I know is: Not my father's. Used to be I knew I was on my Little Master's—that was my one and only side, but now I'm not so sure.

"At least no surcingle. At least a nice long scar." (And he can't even see hardly half of it.) "Misbehave, did you?"

I don't dare say I got it saving a baby Hoot. I change the subject. I tell him I'm looking for my mother.

"Who hasn't lost a mother?" He puts his knife in its scabbard and sits down on the edge of the pool, still blowing every now and then—as if it'll take a while for him to get his breathing back to normal. I sit, too, but not too close.

"Do you know her name?"

"Of course."

"Some don't."

"She's on my registration."

"Some never had any registration and some lost theirs, and some had theirs forged to something better." He looks me up and down then, taking in my conformation. Nods a half-dozen times. "Pure Seattle," he says. Then, "Well, you can't help it."

That's the first time I've heard *anything* like that, as if I'm not the best there is.

I want to say, "And *you* can't help it you're just a Tennessee," but I don't. I say, "I'm out of Merry Mary. My grand-Sue on my father-side was Tutu. You must have heard of her. She was a champion . . . *the* champion, one hundred thirty-two, year of Hoots."

The more I talk about who I am, the more I hate my father. How are we going to have shows and races with everything smashed and Hoots all dead? I was going to live up to my granddam's reputation. All the Hoots said I should, and that I had the conformation to do it, too. I might even be better. Now my father's made it so I'll probably never be able to do what I was born for. Little Master and I, all grownup and "go, go, going," my nose fixed nice and straight and Little Master in his shiniest whites . . . his gold flags. . . . My father was born for it, too, and he didn't even care. If he got to be one of those in that spiky tack, it *was* his own fault. I know it was. I'll bet he had that crazy look of his even before they did all that to him. I don't see why that Tennessee Sue likes him. Far as I'm concerned, he's of even less worth than she is.

"I've seen pictures of Tutu. I can see her in you. And Beauty! Was he your father? I saw him race once! The best!" Then he looks me up and down, my scars, and says exactly what I'm thinking. "You'll not get a chance to be an endurance racer now, for lots of reasons, but some day you could run for us runners. You can carry lots more than I can."

"I *will* be a racer. I'll find a way."

Now he really does look suspicious. "Maybe."

Some place there has to be Hoots living as they used to, in freedom and elegance and hard work and not wasting time. (Like I'm doing right now.) My kind couldn't have ruined *all* their towns.

"Well. . . ." He stretches and breathes another big breath. "I'll keep an eye out for your mom. Where do you live?"

I just stand there. I'm thinking how I wonder where I live, myself. Not any place.

He gives another of those big, sloppy breaths. "I have to go, but I run this route every week, and I always drink right here." He looks at the sun. "About this time, too. You could write me something. Leave it under a rock. Under there, where your dry cakes are. My name is Brandy. What's yours?"

I still can't say anything. Besides, am I Smiley or Charley? Smiley's on my registration.

"So . . . well . . . good luck. I hope your cookies dry."

He starts off at a nice, easy, long-distance, Seattle kind of pace. Halfway down the avenue (it still looks like an avenue, though full of debris), he turns and waves, calls back, "Merry Mary. I'll keep asking."

I wave hard—with both hands. I'm trying to make up for not saying good-bye.

I take another drink and then sit where the runner sat and eat one of the soggy cakes. I'm so hungry I don't care how gummy it is. (These days I'm always hungry. Before, with the Hoots, they made sure I had plenty of everything that would keep me growing, so I'd be the size I'm supposed to be. After a workout, I'd guzzle down a whole quart of milk or juice at one time. Sunrise always looked as if she couldn't believe I could do that.)

Then I think I'll go see how Little Master is getting along without me. I actually miss him. Well, I always did, every time we weren't together. And I start to worry that he might be in trouble. If any Sams or Sues see him, he's done for. Unless *they're* done for.

I go back carefully. I've heard tales of how Hoots can leap down on you and make you their host for life in a half a minute. They did that all the time when they first came. They're good at climbing because of their hands. Funny though, their houses are always half-underground (the tops of them look like igloos, except they go on and on, one room after another after another), but Hoots like to be up high when they're outside and not riding somebody.

When I get close to where I left him, I start being even more careful. I don't want him dropping down on me from any of the Hoot light poles.

I find him on the stall roof, lying flat as he can. (Hard to make that big head look flat, but easy to flatten that body.) There isn't anything to hang on to, and he's grabbing at a tiny metal edge of the ridge pole. Trembling. Scared. And talk about droopy! When he sees me, he perks up a bit, I see it in his ears, but he just stays there.

"Let go," I say. "Slide down. I'll catch you."

But he can't let go. I've heard of that happening, especially with young ones, but I never saw it before. I'll have to go up and pry him loose. Maybe I won't be able to. I'll have to make him feel less scared when what I really want to do is scold him. I want to say, "You almost gave me the 'leap-and-choke.' I saw you. *I'm* the one who's scared." But instead I say—nice and calmly, "Everything's all right now that I'm here. Look how wet I am. I can take you where there's water. Just let go."

"I'm trying."

"Think how you'll ride me. Think how I'll keep you safe."

"I want a mother. I can't let go without one of my mothers."

"I don't know where any mothers are. You have to let go. There's no other way."

But he hangs on.

"Remember how I saved you? Look. Look at my scars." I pull up my tunic and vest, all the way to my shoulders, and then I lift my worst leg towards him, the one with the long scar slanting all the way down. I pull my leggings aside. "Look. What I did for you. I didn't birth you, but I gave you your life back. *I'm* like a mother."

That doesn't work either. I'm going to have to climb up and try to pry him off.

"Put your head down on your hands. Relax all over. You're safe now. I'm coming up."

I'm worrying so much about him, I forget to worry about how he could kill me with these exact same hands, grab me and not be able to let go. He's held me too tight before. That's one of the things our trainer had to keep yelling at him not to do.

But . . . well, do I want my Little Master or not? What would I do down here all by myself? Sleeping without his leg around me and his warm baby breath on my cheek?

I climb on up.

I don't try to pry him off. I lie down beside him and stroke him. I even do a little of their kind of nibbling. I talk mother-talk. I remind him about the doll of me he wants and how, as soon as we get down, we'll go get that. Except we'll go have a drink first and eat a soggy dry cake. I try to make him laugh about our cakes. I tell him how it'll taste so bad he'll say, yuasch, yuasch. His ears go up a little bit. Then I tell him how he'll ride on me and the Smiley doll will ride on him. "Won't that look funny, one of me riding you? And off we'll go, go, go."

That's what finally does it. His ears begin to wiggle-giggle.

He wants to help me dig into his house, but he gets in the way. I put him on a nice smooth piece of unbroken wall to watch me work. He droops, but he perks up when I tell him, "Your job is to listen and smell and look all around in case of danger. That's always a big help." I spread out our half-dry dry cakes again. I say, "Don't let any mama ducks get them."

Breaking the stucco off his house is easy, but I have to find a joint in the mesh to pry it aside, which means I have to pull a lot of stucco off. Even when I find a joint, it's not easy to pry it apart. My father could do that, no trouble at all.

When I finally make a hole big enough to crawl through, I go up beside Little Master and lie back to rest. We each eat half a dry cake. But it looks like he sneaked a couple while I was working. I should have warned him we're going to run out pretty soon. I ought to talk to him about a *lot* of things.

"This is serious. I have to talk to you. You got scared without me, but I got scared, too. You could kill me by mistake even, not even trying. That wouldn't do you much good. Remember our trainer telling you, 'Loose, firm hands? Loose elbows?' If you want to ride me, you have to promise a lot of things. You have to remember, if I'm not safe, you're not either. If I'm not safe, you're as good as dead."

"And *you* have to remember I'm His Excellent Excellency, About-To-Be-The-Ruler-Of-Us-All."

"More likely *I* am. Look at who my father is."

"There never was a Sam who could get to be ruler. And, anyway, I'm trained for it."

"You're just a baby and you know it. You need me a lot more than I need you."

"*Do not.*"

"I don't need you *at all.*" I get up and start walking away.

"And I don't need your dumb doll."

I see him scrabbling up the broken roof of his house, trying to get high again, ears drooping.

"I do. I do. I need you. I know I do."

"So you've finally got that through your stupid Sammish head?" But that's their kind of talk. I change it. "Stupid Hoot head."

"All us Hoots are smarter than any of you. They said you Sams and Sues would eat our brains if you had the chance so you could get as smart as us."

"*Smart!* Is it so smart for you to threaten your one-and-only mount? Maybe one-and-only forever. Where will you get another?"

In the sun, when the light is just right, those great big eyes of theirs look so transparent. You'd think you could see right into their brains and see their thoughts swirling around. And they're such a pale, pale blue. . . .

I wait and let him think. Then I hear his ears flap, giggling again. "I'll ride my Smiley doll," he says.

"Just remember a thing or two."

"Peace and kindness is a Hoot's way."

"Promise? Cross your heart?"

"Promise, but not hope to die."

That'll have to do for now. Besides, I'm anxious to go in.

"Come on. You crawl in first. I'll be right behind. But you think about what I told you."

Inside it's not as squashed as it looked from the outside, though I have to lean over even more than when I was here rescuing

Little Master. And there's light. They have these glowing strips that turn on by themselves if it's dark, and some are still working.

I forgot how grand it is—grand, even all broken. We . . . my own kind, destroyed all this elegance: Plaster underfoot along the halls, pictures on the floor, broken mirrors (they have a lot of mirrors), dead flowers in smashed vases, plant stands tipped over, plants dead . . . but they have a lot of phony flowers, too, bigger and better than any real ones I ever saw. (Maybe they're copies of ones from their planet. They always say, except for us, things were better where they come from.) There's lots of twisted frames, gold and silver, broken but still glittery. That's what you notice most: The shine of everything.

Little Master wobbles off on his skinny legs right away, but, just like that first time, I can't do anything but stare. There's so much I didn't notice before: The handles along the walls and ceilings, black filigree and shaped as if a slot for each finger (that's another thing, they love filigree), the glittery white rugs, here and there on the floor and here and there on the walls, too, and even on the ceiling. (We never had rugs. We had cement floors they had us hose down once a week.) There's my picture and my father's, slanting sideways now, and, further along, my mom's. She's *so* beautiful. Her shiny black hair is in a fancy complicated roll—sort of a filigree look to it, too. *Her* nose is perfect. I don't know if it was ever fixed or not, but I don't think it needed to be. Her legs are muscled. She's wearing short shorts that show them off. She has a perfect conformation. My father didn't love her, even so. Not even *ever!* He practically said so.

I go look at myself in a big cracked mirror. I do look like

my father. I pull my vest up to get a better look at my scars. All my life I tried to be a good Seattle, but now I really do look as if I misbehaved.

Little Master comes rolling back on a baby stool just his size, with his doll of me, and with a pile of nice shiny whites folded into squares. "Look! I found my best whites! If you find silks, we'll look good."

(He doesn't like his scratchy sheep-colored handknit vest any more than I like mine, but we do like how they're warm.)

That doll is so worn-out I wonder how he can still want it. He's hugging it and nibbling at it and licking it like he nibbles and licks me. It's already been licked too much. Pretty soon it'll be licked right through. There are shiny patches on its cheeks and nose. I can't believe it, they made it with a nose just like mine. You'd think they'd have made it so it would look like me *after* I have my nose fixed.

Of course, who cares what my nose looks like up there in the mountains? And I'll bet my father likes his nose just the way it is, just like he likes everything handmade and hard to do—a handmade, hacked-out nose. Little Master will laugh when I tell him.

"*I'm* ready. Can we bring my stool?"

I turn away and unclip my mom's picture from the wall. The picture hangs almost to the floor and it's creased and scratched. That reminds me of her poling. I think how now I know how much that hurt and how she has to wear her misbehavior right out in front like I have to.

I turned away from Little Master because I'm too tired to even *think* about bringing that metal stool. Of course Little

Master doesn't understand about carrying things. He never had to carry one single thing in his whole life—except this doll.

Little Master and I have to talk about a lot more things. It feels safe in here. I'll do it here. While I talk I'll be able to look around. Maybe I should get myself a silver surcingle. Lots of Wild Sams and Sues have them. Except I heard my father say it's like a dog showing off a jeweled leash. We have a dog up there. Hoots hate them. They got rid of most of them first thing. They can't stand how they smell even for a minute. They'd rather smell something dead than a live dog.

We always joke that the Hoots smell bad to the dogs, too, but Hoots say they don't have a smell and how that makes them safe unless seen and heard. And that that makes them better than all the smelly creatures on this world. Anyway, they wouldn't fit comfortably on dogs like they fit on us. Our shoulders are as if made for them. And dogs are too dumb. Hoots are used to smart hosts. Except they often say we're not quite smart enough to know what's in our best interests. I guess we aren't. I guess all this dumb destroying my kind is doing proves it. *I'm* smart, though. I haven't destroyed a single thing nor stolen until this picture of my mom.

I pick Little Master up and take him to his crib. I carry him like the mothers do their infants, by the skin at the back of the neck. They do it so as not to get grabbed by the babies when they don't want to be grabbed. I do it for the same reason, and as a kind of lesson about how I'm in charge now. That crib has glassy-like sides so you can look in at your baby. He can't climb out by himself and I don't have to *ever* take him out unless and until *I* want to.

"I have to tell you more things."

"Praise is better than punishment," he says, ears pricked out towards me, curious.

Our trainer used to try to teach him things practically every minute: To let me breathe and let me see; not to lean over too far, side-to-side or backwards, so as not to get me off balance and maybe make me fall; to "take more care of your mount than you do of yourself. . . ." I've heard our trainer tell him . . . *yell* this at him . . . all these things a hundred times.

"This is about safety." I yell it like a trainer. "For both of us. You have to promise things. Remember cross your heart and hope to die? *Hope to die!*" I say. "*Or else!*"

Chapter Five

He has said enough so that Charley will be safe: Never put your feet where you can't see them. Never reach into any holes or under any rocks. Listen for rattlesnakes. You can eat crawdads. Nothing poisonous resembles chanterelles. You can dry them in an hour on a hot afternoon.

He sits on a stone. The foxes appear—as if out of nothing. They've been there all the time, but so perfectly the colors of the brush it takes stillness to see them. Stillness in him; *they're* already still. A vixen and three kits. The runt is the boldest. Perhaps she has to be. Comes a yard from him if he's careful not to look straight at her. After a few minutes the mother thinks: That's enough of that, and signals her back. One bark. More like a meow. So like cats, they are, climbing into the lower branches of trees.

He would like his life to be this. Sitting silent. Watching. Listening.

He'll keep the vixen's den as one of his secrets—something

of his own that can't be owned. He has learned not to try to hold on to a treasure. It will be taken from him no matter how small or insignificant. Best to own a view. Best to own the smell of pine. And this.

He cries, but it's not much more than heavy breathing—a series of sighs and grunts. For Tutu? For Charley? For Jane (his Bright Spot), because he'll either be off . . . (there's Merry Mary to find) or he'll be chasing after Charley, racing away from Jane as he's doing now.

But no, all this sighing is most likely for himself.

He and Charley could watch the foxes together someday. Share the treasure. Nothing would need to be talked about.

He'd thought to have time to make Charley understand. Keep him from getting to be what he himself had become, so that Charley would never have to do what he'd been forced to do against his fellow human beings.

Fellow human beings can't be said to be his fellows anymore. Why should he be allowed to be as if he was still a person among people? Maybe he ought to stay away from Charley. From Bright Spot, too. From the one and only dog up there. From cats. Nothing around that might lick him, or follow him, or sit on his lap and purr. Rather, something wild to watch. Something that lives as it must. Does what it must and *only* what it must. Never forces another to be cruel to its own kind. Even to its friends. Even to its own mother!

Tutu, worn-down, worn-out. . . . They should have let her rest long ago. When she had finally refused them, he'd been the one to come after her, to bang her against the wall, step on her feet with his metal-soled boots, though he tried not to. Fell against her, trying not to.

They'd planned that on purpose, that the son should come for the mother. Mouth so full of metal he couldn't speak. Couldn't even say, "Mother. Mother." But she must have known.

(Always silence in the stalls of the Sams who hosted the guards. Some couldn't speak at all, but nobody wanted to, anyway. As host to the *head* guard, he was the worst of any of them.)

"I need to go by myself," he'd said to Jane.

"I'll be right behind you."

He will have to say more. She never likes it when he doesn't. "But . . . but. . . ."

"Talk all you want, there's nothing you can say that will stop me following after you."

"Who knows what's . . . *who's* down there?"

"I care about Charley, too."

He doesn't want Charley to change his mind, suddenly, at the worst possible time and place. But maybe nothing for it except that Charley will have to learn the hard way—the hardest way, as he, himself, had. Let Charley make his own mistakes in his own time and way.

Now the long, long view of the valley below. Good for the eyes to see as far as this, into the green and gray and gold. . . . (Red of buckwheat. Red of fox chest.) Good colors for the eyes.

And good for the feet to walk along these paths.

Jane had said she'd come. "With, or ten yards behind. Take your pick."

They'd started last night. Fast . . . a Tennessee's pace. Her pace. They were down into the forested part, at the halfway house by dark.

She'll wake soon. Perhaps she already has and has made squaw tea from the bushes along the trail.

His good Jane. His only Bright Spot. He had never encouraged her, not wanting to be her unreliable bearish lover. Teeth. He still has most of his except for the ones knocked out on each side to make room for the bit.

Her hands next to his. . . . He would never have been allowed to love someone so small. He's gross. All over. Scars, tattoos, misshapen lips.

Once he'd left the print of his fingers on her arm by mistake. Five bruises. She'd tried to hide it.

"Where else have I hurt you without knowing it?"

Now she's by the halfway hut with nobody to drink her tea.

He could leave her there.

Of course not.

But . . . yes. Be alone. She knows the way as well as he does. And she knows him. He can start from here—from the fox's den. Go over the cliff on the far side by himself. She wouldn't want a steep climb, anyway.

He doesn't think, he just does.

And there *is* a kind of happiness left after all. To move his body. Feel his muscles. Look out at the view—down there in fox colors. (He wonders that they call them *gray* foxes.) You can count on the view. You can count on rocks. Well, usually . . . this one he hugs as he climbs down.

First thing after he finds Charley, he will give him his hunting knife. He should have done it before. Charley might need it, what with that baby Hoot on his shoulders.

Jane will come by the east trail, following the river, while he comes straight down, over whatever there is—straight to the fountain.

Whistle back to the birds. You can count on the birds. Startling blue sky. Last night, startling, starry black. Jane *is* a Bright Spot every way there is. Her freckles. The color of her hair, which is the color of the fox's underbelly.

All the sweet, sweet words of loving Jane.

He's hardly ever said them.

Let her speak close into his ear as if a Hoot was telling which way to go. Someday—and he looks forward to it—there'll be no direction to face without Jane to say which way.

Can't Charley see! Their own heads on their own shoulders? (Before Hoots, they used to say, "Two heads are better than one." Now it's "One head is better than none." But what's *that* supposed to mean?)

He'd been exactly the same as Charley, trying to be the best there is, winning prizes. (At Charlie's age, how long would it have taken him to change his mind if someone said, "Change your mind right now?") Later, bought and sold and bought and sold. They'd lied about him, his scars painted over, even the racing numbers tattooed on his upper lip erased and rewritten. Though everybody knew who he was by then. By then an incorrigible. Or was that later? At first he'd been proud of those numbers. Only racing Sams and Sues had them.

Only those few who won *all* the time (as he did) were studs.

Charlie's right, Merry Mary was a sweet woman. Merry when she could be. Sometimes she laughed at herself even in the middle of her crying. (He'd said her name should be "I'm being silly": She said it so often as she cried.) Under the circumstances he couldn't have loved her. There wasn't time for love. They had to do what was expected. Twice in three years, they'd had their four weeks. They'd clung together—especially that first time. There never had been anybody else to hold on to. Not since Tutu. Perhaps Merry Mary had loved him, but he had not loved her. There wasn't any point in it.

He'll tell Charley if he's willing to go back to their mountain village and stay put there, he'll go after Merry Mary right away. How odd it would be—to see her again.

He scares Charley. He can see that. Other people, too. He doesn't feel scary. Just the opposite. He would be the one to hide if he could. Creep around. Be small. Hide behind his own body. Inside his skin. Beyond his scars.

Hide behind Loco Weed. There's plenty at the edge of the Hoot fields. But not now. Later there'll be time for Loco Weed.

It's this life, has to be lived now.

One way or another.

Chapter Six

*L*ittle Master wants to spend the night here, but it's too closed-in—worse than it used to be now that the ceiling's halfway squashed down. Little Master likes it low and cozy, but not me. There's only that one way out, and it's as hard to squeeze out as it was to squeeze in. Even for him, but especially for me.

It *is* wonderfully elegant, and I do like nice things around me. I don't want to live like my father wants to and wants me to—even wants me to *want* to. When I was up there, sometimes I just ached and ached for one or two nice things, and I don't mean just useful things like refrigerators and heaters.

When I grow up I'm going to live in a civilized way no matter where I am, with clean, smoothed-out fingernails, and shiny clothes, hair in a fancy hairdo, and nice, neat eyebrows. (Not like my father's.) I'm going have a stall with pictures of Seattles and a flag on top in the colors of my silks. (I'm too young to have silks now, but as soon as I get to race in real races I'll have them.) Everything beautiful, everything the best, including me.

But I'm not going to spend the night here, so hemmed in. Besides, there's no crib even half my size, and I wouldn't like being in a crib in a cubby anyway.

We spend the night in the stall that's closest to the pond. This time I finally do get some sleep. Partly because we sleep under a cot instead of on it and we hide behind our bundle of stuff so I feel safer. We have a pretty big bundle. I took my mom's picture out of the frame and rolled it to make it easier to carry. I wanted the silver frame so badly, but it's too awkward. I let Little Master bring two of his whites, though they won't stay shiny for long.

Little Master wakes up all droopy. "I dreamed my house," he says, "all closed in, nice and low and cozy, everything curved and round and white, and my cubby curved over me and smooth, shiny clothes, and I dreamed six mothers, but everything fell into little pieces of dry cake, even the mothers. Then you were there, but you were soggy and you fell to pieces, too."

"I'm here. I'm whole." At first I don't say, "Long as you behave yourself," but then I think I should, and then I do. I know I talk too much. I've picked up a lot of bad habits up there in the village. I'm wondering if I'll ever be a proper mount again. I'm not sure I *could* keep quiet anymore. *All* this is my father's fault.

I stroke Little Master for a bit. And pretty soon he pats me and strokes me, too. And nibbles and licks me. Sometimes that's nice, but right now I'd rather he didn't.

Pretty soon, though, we wonder where we ought to go next. Neither of us wants to go back there in the cold and wild where everything is up or down, and lumpy. Little Master couldn't go more than a yard or two even if he had a stool up there. And there's nobody there but Wild Sams and Wild Sues even though lots of them used to be Tames and well-trained. Jane was born Tame, imprinted at birth, too, but she got taken up there when she was seven. She's as bad as any of them, so I guess good imprinting doesn't always matter.

We decide to head for the unknown. We don't care which unknown it is. (We'll have everything we want, at least what's most important to *us*, with us.) Every direction except up into the mountains is unknown. What we'll do is, we'll just head out on any road we like the looks of. We'll get to walk through those tiny red flowers again. They're all over.

Then I think we should go look for Merry Mary, but that's just as unknown as the just *plain* unknown, so we'll go along with whatever road we like best that's not towards the mountains.

I load myself up (I tied our bundle into a kind of knapsack), then I squat for Little Master. He has trouble mounting because he won't let go of his doll, but that turns out to be a good thing, since, just before he's mounted, we hear funny noises. Far away but coming closer fast. We go to the door of the stall and take a look. First we see far away dots and dust, but pretty soon we see a whole batch of mounted Hoots. They're guards. Sounds like them, too, their mounts with iron soles, big, black boots and clanky tack. I know all about them, but I've never seen any except those few that came for Sunrise, and they weren't dressed so fancy.

"They'll smell me for sure," I say.

But Little Master says they won't. "Lie down and don't move. Moving makes you smell more. I'll spread my whites over you, and then I'll lie on top, but first I'll pee along the doorway."

"Can I have an eyehole?"

"A little one, but *don't move!*"

So I get to see them going by, all the Hoot guards in shiny whites and wide black hats, so wide they cover both mount and rider. Us Sams (they're all Sams) are in red, and the tack is shiny red and shiny black. There's lots of silver. Their feet make a wonderful ringing sound. They trot in ranks. Nice and easy, but fast, arms swinging over their chests, all at exactly the same angles. And all the Sams are the same height, too, and they all have black hair. (It could be dyed.) And they all have exactly the same black curled-up-at-the-sides mustaches. Maybe those are dyed, too. A matched company. The Hoot guards are singing. I hear it, but mostly I feel it beating in my head and in my backbone. . . . Every now and then I hear our kind of words: "Go, go, go," and, "sturdy," and, "steady," as part of their song. The Sams' feet are in time with each other, and the Hoots are singing to their beat.

Then there's three big sparking bangs. The chuck, chuck, chuck, *bang!* That's when the Hoots have the poles set on highest. The Hoot out front is throwing out fire balls from his pole.

This is the most wonderful thing I've ever heard or seen in my whole life! This is *perfect!* Better even than when they have shows with us in our silks and flags all over, and those of us who play piccolo, play. (They like the piccolo best of all our instruments.)

I want to go with them. I want to be one of those Sams. They could train me. I'd do everything just right. I make a move to get up, but Little Master gets a Hoot grip on me. (One big hand curls my leg tight in, and the other pulls my arm behind me. That hurts.) I was going to yell anyway, but then I see the gleam on the silver cheek-pieces of their bits, and I think about my father with a tooth knocked out on each side, and scars. I can imagine what must be *inside* their mouths. Or I can't. These are, all of them, like my father, the very worst of us Sams. The incorrigible. The untrainable. And I *am* trainable. I wouldn't get along with them any better than I get along with my father.

So Little Master and I wait, utterly still, and listen. . . . And listen and listen till way after we can't hear them anymore. Seems like they're on their way up the mountain. Towards us Sams and Sues up there. Towards all those people I don't like— but towards Sunrise, too. And Jane. . . . I don't like her, but she really tries to be nice.

The more things that happen, the more I don't know which side I'm on.

Even as Little Master was hanging on to me, I was wondering: Why is he holding me back? And how did he know all that about peeing? Wouldn't he rather they rescued him? But he was scared, too. I could tell by the way he was holding me, and, after they go by, and he sits back, I see his ears swiveling all around, listening still, though everything's quiet.

"What did you do all that for?"

"I don't know."

"Aren't you Hoots all kind and generous? You were scared. What are you scared of? And how did you know that about peeing?"

"That's a known thing. We all know that."

"Don't you want to get rescued and back with your own kind?"

His ears go straight out sideways when I say that. That always makes him look funny. I laugh, and then he laughs because I do.

"You don't know, do you?" I say. "I mean I'm all mixed up and you are, too."

Then we get quiet and just sit and think. Actually, I *don't* think. My brains won't work. I just keep still and look at my shoes. Then I do think, but about shoes. If I don't find a bigger pair pretty soon, I'll have to wear homemade. That isn't what I want to be worrying about right now. Little Master has his doll on his lap and gives it a lick now and then. I'll bet he's not thinking, either.

All of a sudden I find myself saying, and I don't know why, "I have to go back." I didn't even know I was going to say that.

He doesn't say yes or no, or good or bad, or anything, he just hugs his doll and gets ready to mount.

We start for the pond to drink and to eat some of our cakes, but when we get close—for heaven's sake, I see my father! Sitting there on the rim of the pond, calm as could be—or, rather, calm as always. (He's stuck in always being calm.) He just keeps sitting, watching us come. When I think back about when I first met him, I remember he was even calm when he poled me. Even after he poled me, he was still completely calm. You'd think somebody with as many scars and tattoos and lips out of shape could never be calm.

He waits. He doesn't think we'll turn and run away, and we don't. Little Master's ears are so far out in front I see the tops. I can read his curiosity right from here, underneath.

I'm being calm, too. I walk right up and sit down on the wall. Not too close, though.

We sit. All he says is, "Charley." No, it's "Ch . . . Ch . . . Charley," as usual. He's glad to see me. (I *think* he is. I wish he had a face that showed more. He's like a statue.) And I feel . . . well, not exactly glad, but relieved to see him. Little Master's ears are still way, way forward. He's not worried, he's wondering. Which is funny: He was scared of his own kind going by, but he's not scared of my great big lumpy father, even though my father tried to kill him.

Everything is getting so mixed up, I don't ever want to think any more at all. And I'm not.

I look sideways at my father. Kind of out of the corner of my eye so he won't notice. I'm imagining him as one of those guard mounts. I can see that in him—that kind of perfection, glitter and all. I'd like to ask him about it, like what *did* he have in his mouth, *exactly?* But maybe he wouldn't want to be reminded.

After a while I ask, "Did you see *them?*" *That* can't hurt him to answer.

"I saw."

I guess that's all he's going to say about it.

We sit. Just sit. Little Master and I are thirsty, but we don't drink. It's as if we're still scared, but in a different way, like nothing bad is going to happen, but we don't dare move around too much.

But pretty soon along comes Jane. At a trot. She has a lot to carry. I don't know why my father let her have all the bundles.

First she says, "*Charley!*" And then, "I was worried," and then, "about *all* of you."

I'm thinking it's silly to worry about my father.

First she hugs my father, then she hugs me. She even gives Little Master a couple of strokes on his fuzzy red hair (it's just baby fuzz and much redder than hers). I know for sure she didn't want Little Master around us all the time up there, except she did get used to him, but she's sort of like Sunrise, she doesn't care what you are. I guess that goes along with her liking my beat-up old father. She doesn't care what he looks like and even that he can hardly talk. Then she asks if we're hungry, and all of a sudden we're not scared to move around anymore. Something about Jane makes everything all right. Little Master dismounts, and we both lean over the edge of the pond and drink. When we lean back up, Jane is spreading out food, even greens for Little Master. She says she picked them on the way down and boiled some for her breakfast.

She asks us, did we see the flowers?

Little Master's ears look giggly again. "I sang them!" He shouts it. "I sang them *all!*"

"Bright Spot," my father says and grabs Jane's hand and makes her sit beside him. He only calls her that for special. He says, "Sorry." I don't know what for, and then, "Did you use your . . . smell kit?"

She says, "It's all right." And, "I wasn't worried." (They always have these conversations that I don't know what they're talking about, but I'll bet it has something to do with Jane ending up with all the bundles.) She leans her head against his shoulder. I'm thinking: But what about Merry Mary? I squat down and unroll Merry Mary's picture and spread it in front of them. They both look at her really hard. I say, "My mother," just in case my father forgot what she looked like.

Jane says, "Beautiful!" as she should, seeing as how Jane is just a skinny freckled. I feel a little bit sorry for her, but I'm glad my mom is so beautiful. To my father I say, "You promised you would find her."

But he doesn't answer. He turns to Jane and pulls her face around so she's looking at him. He says, "Beautiful," right to her, and then he takes her hand and kisses it, hard, like he wants her to know he really means it, and, still staring at her, says, "Beautiful," twice again.

Well, that's nice of him, but *everybody* can see she isn't.

Then he turns to me. "They have. . . . The people . . . gone. . . ." Then he coughs out a big "*Kh! . . . Cliffs!*"

I know he means the people will be up there in the secret place, and no guards could follow except one-by-one. Then he says, "Merry Mary . . . yes . . . but first. . . ."

Then all of sudden he *can* talk, almost like the rest of us.

"I can't leave poor mounts. Like that. Like those. Not leave like that. I can't. I won't."

There . . . that's the first time I've ever seen him not calm.

And he says it as if there's no doubt in his mind that he can save them, that it's all up to him and nobody else. I guess maybe it is, but I do doubt. I counted them. It'll be him . . . just one Wild Sam against twenty . . . twenty-one, it was . . . and all just about as big as he is, and all those Hoots had poles.

Then he looks at us in an odd way. Thinking hard. "Ch . . . Charley. . . . I'll need you. You'll have to let Little Master ride Jane for a while."

He shouldn't have said that. Little Master, squatting beside me, gets a Hoot hold on my elbow and my wrist.

My father takes the knife that's buckled to his belt. (That belt is really, more or less, a surcingle, but he wouldn't want to hear it called that.) For a minute I'm worried about Little Master, but my father takes everything, belt and all, and buckles it around my waist. First, though, he has to use the knife to make another couple of holes so it'll fit me.

While he's still got the knife, he says (and back to sputtering), "Do you know . . . what this is . . . for?" Now he holds it low and upside-down like that runner did when he almost cut me.

I shake my head no.

My father makes a motion, his right arm across his chest— up and back, fast and sure. The Hoots have their heads either resting on top of our heads or on our left, cheek to cheek. (The left is the proper side for everything they do.) If he'd had a Hoot on his shoulders, cheek to cheek like that, for sure it would be dead.

I can feel Little Master loosen his hold as though he's getting ready to jump away from me.

I'm thinking how I'll never, never do that, but, right after, I'm also thinking about the leap-and-choke and how he sometimes holds me by my throat; this knife will be a good thing to have—for lots of reasons.

My father buckles it on me so that when I grab it, it'll be upside-down the way he had it.

"What will you do without it?"

He picks up his pole—I hadn't noticed it there, by the wall of the pond. "Fine," he says.

"But if. . . . Those guards?"

"*Fine!*"

He never talks much, but when he does it thumps down and lies there by itself. No wonder there was always silence when we ate with the others up at the village.

I see Jane has a pole, too, one of those small ones sticking out of her pack.

After we eat—and for once there's enough, dried meat and parched corn and everything (I didn't ask what kind of meat it was. I didn't want to know.)—they gather everything up (my father takes most of the bundles this time). They smear us with a smelly goo and say we'll get used to it in a couple of minutes, and we head towards the mountains but not following the road. We just go straight out. You can see by the squashed flowers that somebody . . . somebody with big feet—my father, probably—walked this way before, just skuffed along and wasn't even a little bit careful of them.

That smell bothers Little Master a lot more than it does me. I'm wondering if he'll ever get used to it. He keeps leaning back and away, trying to get a breath of fresh air, but then, as we go through the flowers, he starts to kick his feet and sing again. "I'm singing about you, too," he says. Then he starts to bounce, as if I didn't have a nice smooth trot. I hope my father and Jane don't notice and think it's me bouncing. But I feel good, too, anyway. It's still morning and there's all this red—off on each side of us as far as you can see—and I had a good meal and almost got full for a change.

We go straight—practically right straight through the forest. We climb everything that's in the way. We push through brush. We hardly even go around anything, and when we come to the cliffs, where you usually go a mile or two farther down where it's not so steep, my father goes straight up the cliff face. If we weren't with him, he'd be going up just as fast as he walks, I'll bet. He hangs on by the tippy, tippy tips of his fingers and toes. You'd think such a big man wouldn't be able to do that. We can't, and we're not even big. Well, Little Master could, but he won't let go of me. My father helps us, sometimes with a long stick for us to grab on to.

Little Master isn't scared. Hoots are good climbers, and they feel safe when they're on top of something. (Not counting when they feel safe all closed-in underground.) I'm *mostly* not scared either, but Jane is. Rocks are one thing, but we cross a landslide area. You can hear gravel trickling down even when we aren't crossing. That scares all of us . . . except I guess not my father. Or, anyway, he doesn't show it—when does he ever show anything? Jane is shaking. He helps her cross first. He says for her to keep looking at him. (You can see she's all stiff as she hangs on to my father.) Then he comes back for me. He uses the stick stuck in the landslide above us as if to hold back the river of gravel. We get across, but we end up a couple of yards farther down and have to climb up all over again. We had to cross the slide area because the cliff got so it slanted out above us, and my father thought we'd not be able to climb that.

We rest on the far side to get over being scared. We sit and listen to the trickling down, which is even more than before. Jane cries a little bit. I know she's so relieved we didn't fall, and maybe so tired. I feel the same way. She tries to hide it. She turns away from us and wipes her chin with just one finger when the tears get down that far, but my father sees and goes to her and calls her Bright Spot again a couple of times and holds on to her. Little Master says he was scared, too, but I don't think he was. I think he's just being nice to Jane, which is not like a Hoot at all. Well, I'm changing, too. Jane is such a nice person, she's even beginning to look pretty good.

After that crossing, I start getting worried about this whole thing, like what will happen to us when we meet the guards? Maybe I'll get to be a guards' mount without even wanting to anymore. I find a little stick and put it across my mouth to see what a bit might feel like. Little Master says, "Don't do that." Then my father notices and gives me such a wide-eyed look. . . . He opens his mouth to speak, to shout, more likely, but nothing comes out at all, except some choking breaths. He looks as if he's going to have an attack of some sort.

There's something he needs from me—or for me. This is part of what my rescue is all about. I'm supposed to be a certain way. I'm supposed to have a kind of life that has nothing to do with anything he went through. I can't even try to find out what his life felt like. I could drive him crazy. I could not spit the stick out.

My father comes at me, but Jane grabs him. She says "Heron!" but in a whisper, so, so softly. They hang on to each other as if each one is the cliff we're climbing and they'd fall to their deaths in the next minute if they didn't have the other one to hold.

I spit out the stick and look away. I never do like to see them hugging like that right in front of people, though now it's just us.

Even struggling along like this, we're saving a lot of time. We'll get to the top of the first pass before the guards do. And all of us smelling like . . . maybe like dogs. Well, there are so few dogs now, they'll think: Coyotes, or wolves. I hope we smell scary. I wonder if they can tell there's only three of us and one Hoot? They'll be thinking Little Master is in charge. I would. He's getting bigger, too. Last couple of months we both are. Sunrise measured. (She even measured Little Master.) I wonder if I'm twelve yet. It was in my folder, but I forget. Maybe Sunrise can tell.

Those guards will have to spend the night below us. Or maybe they'll go on all night. *We* can't see in the dark, but Hoots can. They wouldn't go as fast, and the mounts would need plenty of leg cues from the Hoots, but they could go, go, go. All us Sams and Sues are good at sensing the slightest movements from our riders. We can even tell where they're looking by their seat on our shoulders. That's what our trainer was always yelling at Little Master: "Look where you're going so your mount will know, too!"

My father stops now and then to let us rest and drink. He's not breathing hard, though he's carrying most of the stuff and all the water. One time when we rest, I say, "The Hoots know there are hardly any dogs left, will they think we're wolves?"

"The smell . . . it's . . . grizzly."

"Bear! Oh, great!"

Then Jane talks for him like she does sometimes, "Mountain lion would scare them more, but bear smell is stronger and easier to get." She's leaning way over against my father, as usual. You'd think he'd be too lumpy for comfort.

"Will they know we're only just us two Sams and one Sue and one Hoot?"

"No."

Little Master doesn't talk much in front of my father, but he says, "They'll know."

We get up to the saddle of the mountain. It's still not late, though the sun is about to set behind one of the far peaks. We're well beyond the halfway hut. It's a mile below us, back towards town.

I flop down—we all do—and look at the sky—which is nothing, not a single cloud. It seems as if none of us has the energy to look anywhere but straight up. After a while, Little Master moves his legs from my shoulders (he's still half on me, and I'm lying against a stone) and finds a softer spot to curl up in. Pretty soon I have the energy to turn and look at all of us, sprawled out there. We're a mess. It's a good thing we all have short hair and don't have to do it up every morning like I used to have to. My hands . . . all our hands are scratched and dirty, front and back. We're dirty all over, with bloody scraped places. Even places you'd never think could get scraped. Our clothes are torn. Even Little Master is dirty and torn. We look completely uncivilized. This is *exactly* what I never wanted to be or be around. I suppose I'll have to call myself a Wild Sam.

When we finally have the energy, we chew on our chewy things. I don't care what anything tastes like. We don't even notice if it has a taste at all. This is not only *exactly* what I never wanted to eat, but *exactly* how I never wanted to eat it. I may be changing—I do feel friendly lying here with them after a scary climb—but I haven't changed how I'd like my life to be. There's something about all this my father does like: Homemade and hardships. After our all-day hike up to the secret town and back, he told me he loved to be all worn out from hiking. "It's a good kind of tired." And I thought, well, I like that, too, but only after a nice race with a Hoot on my back, or a nice hard circling on the go-round so I know I'm getting to be a better mount.

Pretty soon we feel rested enough to start to wonder things again, like (again) will the guards stay in the halfway hut and the mounts have to stay outside? Or will they go on all through the night? The three of us wonder. Not my father, he sits, listening, alert. He doesn't have to be so alert with Little Master here. There's no way he can notice anything before a Hoot would. Even if Little Master wasn't paying attention, he would hear things way before my father could.

Then my father gets up and leaves. He just gets up, without a single word, and walks away. Down. Towards the trail and the halfway hut, where the guards will be, or be on their way to.

Jane and I look at each other. Then she says, "That's how he is. Always is. We'll wait a bit and then we'll follow." Then she calls, "Be careful," but my father's gone. There's nobody but us to hear.

That's what we meant to do, follow in a few minutes, but we're so worn out we doze off. All of us. When we wake up, it's pitch dark. We're up too high for trees, so it must be cloudy because we can't see a single star. It's Little Master tells us my father's still gone. He can see he's not here—and even though we have that bear smell smeared on us, he can smell he's not, too.

Jane says, "Why didn't Heron take Little Master so he could see?" Then she asks Little Master, would he have done it—gone with him and led him through the dark? Little Master says he would for me, and after a minute he says he *might* do it for her, too, but not for my father. "He's too big, and too untamed, and he would take his knife if he had me on him."

"Help us free those Sams," she says. "We can't see anything without you."

"Those Sams are worthless. That's why they're guards' mounts."

She says, "If they're worthless, then we're all worthless."

"I'm About-To-Be-The-Ruler-Of-Us-All. You're just primates. You couldn't hear those things they sang to teach me things even if you listened. They sang me how those mounts were ruined way before they even got to be guards' mounts."

"Heron was one of them, for heaven's sake!"

I can't see anything, but I can hear her swishing about beside me. Even just hearing her move, I can tell she's angry.

"Hoots!" she says.

And then I hear Little Master say, "Kindness is the best policy." And then, "Except when it comes to guards' mounts. They're bad."

We leave our stuff there except for Jane's pole and my knife. I don't want to leave my mother's picture (for a minute I get really scared because I can't find it in the dark, but Little Master sees it and gives it to me). Little Master doesn't want to leave his doll, but Jane says it'll be safer if we don't carry it with us. Little Master finds us a good place under an overhanging rock. I say, "What about rattlesnakes?" but Jane says, "They'll be too cold. Besides, I think we're up too high." We put everything under that rock, the food packs and water, and cover them with stones. Jane smears a little bear cream around them.

We start down slowly. We could have Jane's pole lit just a little bit for light, but we don't want to be noticed, so all we have is Little Master telling us what to step over and what to go around. We're trying to be quiet, but we stumble a lot. Jane and I hold hands when we can.

We think we're pretty quiet, but Little Master says we're making a terrible racket. Pretty soon he says he smells things close by, and we should stop and wait, and no whispering, while he listens. We squat down and don't move. We leave it all up to him.

"It's your father," he says. "He's close to us and to them, too. If I know he's there, then so do they."

I say, "But they think he's a bear."

"He's got a lot of his own smell on him. I noticed that before. He's not like Jane—or you, either. Since all of us Hoots are smarter than any of you, after they smell him, none of us will think that any of you are bears."

We hear whistling then. It's those whistles that they never would tell me what they meant. (I ought to be old enough to know by now.) And then answering whistles. After that there's shouting and crashing around in the brush. And all of a sudden we can see—clear as day. Fires are all around. Even though there's not that much brush, it's oily, dry-climate kind of brush and burns easily. I didn't know it could flare up so high.

We stand, not even trying to hide. Not that there's a place for it. Maybe a boulder or two among the brush. Below us, there's a ring of fire almost all the way around the halfway hut. Those big, black-haired mounts are jumping all over the place, but they're hopping in an odd way. Then I see they're hobbled. Their hands are tied, too. Huddled on top of the hut are the Hoot guards. I don't know which side set the fires, but now the Hoots are sending off fireballs all over the place. One fizzles right above our heads and ashy stuff flakes down on us. Everything crackles.

Then I see my father—leaping a great leap—a black shadow silhouetted against the fire. It's more a Tennessee leap than a Seattle leap. I can't tell if he's on fire or not or if it's just his pole, spitting out sparks all around him.

I grab my knife and follow. I leap a big leap, too. I can feel how much I'm like him. I even whistle. I don't know what I want it to mean, I just want to do it. I still don't even know which side I'm on, not for sure. I still want to be well-trained and civilized. I still hate the way they live up here. I hate being all scratched and dirty, but I keep whistling signals I make up on the spot and jump right into the middle of things. I don't know what's going on and I don't even care. I want to be part of it just like I wanted to be one of the guards' mounts. I don't know what I'm going to do. I'll just do whatever comes along.

Above me, on me, Little Master is making a racket, too. I can only hear a little of it, but I can tell it's a loud, high, crazy song. I wonder what the Hoot guards will be thinking of it?

Right in front of us there's three mounts with their hands tied and then tied to each other. We bump right into them. They look shiny and scary, even those big black mustaches make them look scary, but they're hobbled and tied, and I'm the one with the knife.

There's one practically nose-to-nose with me. For a minute I stare into his eyes. I'm thinking how they're all big, but I'm almost . . . *almost* eye-to-eye with him. Time seems to stop, and I see—something that isn't ever in my father's eyes—there's a brightness—there's hope. That guard can't be a lot older than I am. His mustache is just painted on, or, more likely, tattooed. I want a mustache tattooed on, like his. My father just has numbers on his upper lip. Those numbers don't look good, but this does.

I cut him free. I cut the other two, who are tied to him, all free.

Then I . . . we . . . turn to the hut. The Hoots are on the roof sparking their poles all over us. It's raining prickly fire. We can't see what's happening, with all the smoke and everybody running and jumping all over the place. I'm still not sure what I'm going to do, but Little Master decides for me. He pulls my head to the side and leans way over. That's the sure way to make a mount fall. Easy to do even for a small Hoot, so of course I fall. We go down hard—my elbows and my forehead—and I think Little Master hits his head, too. We both cry out, practically the exact same cry. Afterwards we lie there, getting kicked and stepped on, and Little Master whimpers to himself, his legs still wrapped around my shoulders. I'm thinking, if he wanted to pull me down, this wasn't exactly the best place, right in the middle of everybody jumping on us. I can't even get up. I crawl out from under, towards the dark, as best I can.

As soon as we get away from the ring of fire, I can't see *at all*—that dark is even darker with the brightness behind us— but Little Master says, "Save me that one. Just one. That one. There." And with all this banging and shouting going on, he starts to hum a mother song.

Then my hand touches something warm and trembling—a weak, stick-like leg with no muscles.

They're probably looking at each other, Little Master and this Hoot guard, but I can't see a thing except after-images from the fires.

If those guards' mounts are the worst of *us*, the guards have got to be the worst of *them*. They're the kind of Hoots that pushed Sunrise against the wall and had a mount step on her on purpose.

I still have my knife, clutched so tight all this time I'm not sure I could let go of it if I wanted to. I don't know what to do. Kill the guard or what?

Chapter Seven

It's them, the mounts, who kill the guards. We don't have to. I suppose my father takes part, but I don't want to know about it. Mostly I saw him freeing mounts. But talk about Wild! Last I saw, he looked crazier than ever. He was twirling and twirling his pole around his head, so that it actually blew the Hoots' fireballs away, sent them high above the fight, so far up most of them dwindled and came down as ash. (I wonder how he knew to do that? I hope some day I'll get to do it, too.) The mounts don't actually kill the Hoots, either. The roof of the hut catches fire and they circle it and won't let the Hoots come down. Some Hoots jump and break their legs right away. The roof isn't high, but Hoots' legs are so weak.

Then the walls start to collapse. The hut isn't a real cabin, just an overnight shelter made of brush and thatch and stones and a few logs. Up this high there isn't much decent wood. The ridge poles must have been carried up. The dying Hoots made an odd mewing sound. Probably most of it was too high for us Sams and Sues to hear, but it gave me a funny feeling—

hunched up my shoulders and curled my toes and fingers. I suppose it was the part I couldn't hear that did that. I did let go of my father's knife, but I picked it up again. Except it was as if my hands wouldn't work with that sound going on. My brain wouldn't work, either.

But then it stopped. And I knew they were all dead. (Except for that one Little Master and I hid.)

That's a sound I hope I never, ever, ever have to hear again.

Then it's quiet. Quieter than quiet. Everybody just stands there. Listening to the silence. It's the best silence I ever heard. I'm sure that's what we all feel. Then everybody sits down, more or less right where they already are. It's not dark because fires are still burning, though mostly dying. Here and there, a guards' mount stamps one out and then collapses beside it.

Even though we're sitting down, Little Master and I are getting lots of funny looks from the mounts since I'm the only Sam around that has a Hoot host. I'm worried, and I can feel Little Master's fear in the way he's sitting and hanging on. I see Jane farther up the hill. I put my knife away and move towards her, slowly, so as not to startle any of the mounts.

I have to go past them to get to her. They lie, bruised and sweaty and burned and smudged, but even so, they still look good to me. I'm wishing I had their silver and red tack. Their lacquered hair—and most of their mustaches *are* real. I wonder if my father would grow one if I asked him to. I wonder when *I'll* be able to grow one.

By now they've spit out their bits. There's silver cheek-pieces, side-chains, silver surcingles lying all over the place. All of that tack etched with tiny scenes of mounts, leaping, prancing. I always thought that showed how much they love us Sams and Sues—that they decorated everything, even us, with us.

The mounts let me and Little Master pass.

The farther up the hill I get, the darker it is, but I can see enough to see my father is there, Jane beside him. He's sprawled on his back, legs spread, arms spread, taking up a lot of room. First I think he's dead, and I feel all shivery up and down my spine. I wonder if everything will fall apart now, and I'll have to find Merry Mary all by myself.

I guess Jane can see my look even in this light. "Just passed out," she says. "It was too much for him."

"How could anything be too much for my father!"

I didn't mean to say that out loud, but I do.

Jane is washing him with canteen water and putting that stuff we have on his burns. She stops, though, when I say that.

"Oh, Charley, you have no idea." She leans towards me to try to see me better in these shadows. The fires are down the hill, but a little light flickers on her face even up here—turns her even more reddish than she already is. "Just because a person is big and strong doesn't . . . doesn't mean. . . ." Then she hugs me. I remember Merry Mary's big-around, strong arms and big breasts. Jane doesn't feel at all like her, but, though bony, she feels pretty good, anyway. We stay hugging for a while. She doesn't seem to mind that Little Master is in on it, too, all three of us bunching up together. I see his hands are around her head, but nice and easy, patting like they do for us but never for each other. It's the primate way. Who ever heard of a dog or a cat patting?

I'm glad my father is still passed out. I wouldn't want him to see this. If he was awake, I wouldn't be doing it.

Then, still mostly leaning together, we kind of fall over sideways, all three of us, comforted enough to rest.

Pretty soon we hear my father groan. He starts to come to, so we let go of each other. Jane goes to him, and my father reaches up to her. I turn away, though I can feel, in the twist of his body, that Little Master keeps looking. Then my father gives another big groan, and I hear the rustling of his getting up. It sounds like he doesn't want to. He starts down towards the mounts and the hut. I get up and follow.

Like all the fires, the hut is just smoldering now. All along the way to it, there's just enough light to see the guards are all sprawled out, kind of like my father was. Some are asleep, snoring, and some are looking at the sky. They seem to be waiting for dawn. And just as I'm thinking that dawn is what they're waiting for, here it comes.

My father turns around to watch the light on the mountains opposite from where the sun is about to come up, and I do, too. We watch the little rim of pink broaden from slivers outlining the peaks to red splashes, drowning out the purple. But then, when I turn back, I see my father isn't looking at the mountains anymore, he's looking at me. He reaches to touch me, and I step away. He looks down then, as if he's shy. Even in front of me. You wouldn't think someone so big could ever be shy, especially in front of a child. When I get to be that size, I'm not going to be shy.

My father turns and limps down among the mounts, and I'm right behind. He's all wobbly. Like his knees might buckle any minute. The mounts stand up as he comes by. They know who he is. They say, "It's Heron. Our Heron." They're all . . . *of course* they're all Seattles, but my father is bigger than they are. I knew he was big, but I didn't understand, until right now, how he's even bigger than most Seattles. No wonder I was eye-to-eye with that mount, seeing as who I am. And I can see how the mounts know who I am, too. I guess I don't have a (so far child-sized) big nose for no reason. And my hair flops, sloppy, over my eyes, just like his. (There isn't any hair lacquer up at the village. Besides, up there they're proud of looking Wild.)

But now, even those mounts look pretty Wild—except their hair and mustaches, which the lacquer keeps in place. And they look kind of stunned and dizzy, and, when they get up, they're as wobbly as my father. I see the start of their morning beards. Some are too young, but most are as old as my father. I guess it takes time to misbehave enough to be a guards' mount—for Hoots to give up on you entirely. Like they always say, "Kindness first. Benefits of doubts. Trust. A Sam or Sue may know something you don't. Ask. Love." I heard all those over and over when they shouted them at Little Master, and I took them to heart as much as he did.

The mounts reach out to touch my father as he goes by—he's heading for the burned-up hut. They don't know what to make of me, though, what with Little Master on my shoulders.

I look for that mount I freed first. I wonder what he did so young that was so bad it got him into this much trouble? I'll bet he hasn't even come into his full growth. But the mounts don't like me coming too close with a Hoot on my shoulders, so I keep over to one side.

When my father gets down by the hut—it's not a hut any-more, just a pile of smoky stuff—he doesn't even look at it that I can tell. He collapses down again and puts his arms on his knees and his head on his arms. I'm in no mood for another collapse, and Little Master isn't either. He says, "Come. Go, go, go." And grabs my ear on one side and pushes my cheek on the other and turns my head back towards the hill. That's not at all the proper way to control a Sam, but I let him turn me. We go up, not straight up, but over to the side where there's a big batch of boulders that rolled down from farther up and landed in a depression. According to what my father taught me, a perfect place for rattlesnakes. This is where we hid the Hoot guard. I remember how my father said rattlesnakes don't live above a certain height, but I don't know if this is *the* height. It's still morning and cool. I wouldn't want to go back in there when they've warmed up. (Once my father showed me a place a lot like this where we counted seven, all coiled up together.)

None of us could have seen me hide the Hoot, since I couldn't see anything myself as I did it. I didn't even know for sure this was where he is.

Little Master guides me around behind the rocks and dips me down half under one of the biggest ones, and there's the Hoot, looking small, curled around himself, and his big hands spread out across his stomach for warmth. Hatless, whites no longer white. He looks up at us, blinking those big translucent eyes of his. I see my silhouette and the sky behind me reflected in the milky blue. I almost can read his thoughts back in there. I see him recognize Little Master. "*You!*" he says. "*You! You!*

Future-Ruler-Of-Us-All! I give myself." And then he starts to sing. "Oh best, best. I sing the best there is."

I had almost forgotten how the Hoots are always saying, you. But how does he know it's His Excellent Excellency About-To-Be-The-Ruler-Of-Us-All just in one look?

He takes the pose, one big hand as if shielding his eyes from the sun, as if Little Master is all shiny and white, though he isn't now. And bares his neck to be choked.

Little Master says (to me), "Squat." He says it as though we were back home, and as if he was still in charge of everything, and I do, just as if he was. He climbs off, balancing on my knife belt as though it was a surcingle.

The Hoot says, "I need a host."

"There aren't any." Little Master.

"*Command!*"

"I can't."

I've been keeping my mouth shut like a good Sam should, but then I say, "I'm in charge around here."

He looks us over. It's as if he just noticed our handknit sweaters. Our dirt. I guess, big as I am, he can see my age. After all, they're used to making age judgments when they pick out their mounts. First he says, "You're a Wild," and then he says, "You're not even grownup."

I say, "I'm even almost ready to be a voter."

"Hoots live by kindness and by praise. We don't put fancy names to things, we just do what's right. If you weren't a Wild, you'd know."

I pull my upper lip out and turn it up to my tattoo. I'm too young to have a whole number, but I have the beginning—an

S and a *l* and an *A*. I saw it in a mirror. Later they'll put my racing status. If there is a later.

Then I see him gather his legs under him for the leap-and-choke. I jump back, which wouldn't have done me a bit of good considering how fast Hoots are, but it's not for me he's grabbing, it's Little Master. Right around his neck. "Now!" he says. "Now!" and holds on and stares at me. Little Master is already starting to turn blue.

"He saved you."

"I need a host."

"But he's About-To-Be-The-Ruler."

"I need a Seattle like yourself."

Little Master is getting bluer and bluer. I take out my knife. I may not be fast enough to do much, but he'll have to let go of Little Master to fight me.

Then it's *my* neck he has. So fast I don't know how it happened. I can see prickly blackness coming in from the sides till there's nothing but a little bright spot. Next thing I know I'm on the ground and the Hoot guard is on top of me, dead and bleeding from his mouth. Little Master did it.

The guard didn't get that sort of death hold on us—nothing happened to my Adam's apple or Little Master's, but Little Master went straight for that, first thing.

Little Master pulls the guard off me and then begins to cry. Not just drooping ears, but that high-pitched trembly sound that twangs my backbone.

I shush him. "Stop it. They'll come."

He stops, but they come. My father first. I guess he can see right away what happened. He grabs me and lifts me up and shakes me like I'm a rag, not a Seattle almost as big as he is.

"Whose side . . .? What's this Hoot?"

"I don't know what you're asking." But of course I do.

"Whose?"

He keeps shaking me. Can't he see I only just this minute almost got choked to death? Can't he see I'm still holding the knife? And just the way he taught me? Ready to kill? And how can a person think when they're getting shaken up like this?

"Not *your* side! Not *yours!* I'll never be on your side."

He drops me . . . not drops, throws me down. When my father throws something, it really gets thrown.

"We killed him, didn't we? It was Little Master killed him, but I was going to."

The mounts are crowding around us, and then here's Jane asking me if I'm all right. Asking both of us. And saying, "For heaven's sake," like she does, but to my father this time. "For heaven's sake, your own son."

She helps me up. She even helps Little Master mount. Then she takes my hand and leads us to where our things are and sits us down and gives us drinks and washes our faces.

Little Master droops. He says, "We're each others' only ones," and he won't get off until I say I'll hold him on my lap. I start thinking, Merry Mary, Merry Mary. It's because *I* want to be on somebody's lap, too, but I never get to be.

"Say me," Little Master says. "Say me then. As if a mother. Don't try to sing, just say."

I remember all the things Merry Mary sang and said back when I was little. Those tales and songs were mostly from the time before the Hoots. Till we got up there at the village of

Wilds, I'd never told them to Little Master or anybody. If you'd asked me, I'd have said I'd forgotten all about them. Sunrise didn't tell me any back down home. I was always too tired. Sometimes I heard her humming as I went to sleep. She strummed on a homemade guitar kind of thing. She only did that at night when we were all locked in and the Hoots were in their burrows.

Back there our playtimes were short and our trainer wouldn't have let us tell stories. If there was any singing, our trainer did it. But up at the village we had time. I could remember things, and Little Master and I could sit out someplace by ourselves and talk and tell. First we just talked about how good it used to be back home, and all the things we missed, but then I thought about Merry Mary's tellings. I changed three bears to three Sams or Sues without hosts and one lost baby Hoot wobbling on his skinny legs. I didn't want to scare Little Master with bears. (There really *were* bears around there.) Any princesses I always made into Hoot mothers. Stepmothers I made into wicked trainer mothers.

I turn us away. I say, "Once upon a time," and he puts his arms around me and leans, all relaxed, his cheek against my neck, his damp breath tickling. "Once upon a time a baby Hoot got lost in the woods. He could walk a little bit better than most because he practiced. You could see muscles in his legs. When you squeezed them, they felt like rubber, not like a bunch of loose strings." Little Master grunts and looks up at me, surprised, but then cuddles in again. (I've never said anything like this before, but I've been thinking about leg muscles, how mine are strong because I made them strong on purpose.)

"This little Hoot practiced every day. Secretly. Even his faithful Sam mount didn't know. He didn't dare use the go-round. He had to go round and round by himself.

"One day he was out in the woods practicing going some real place. He was even shouting, "Go, go, go," to himself, and he was go, go, going farther than ever before, because his legs had gotten stronger than even he knew, when he came upon a Wild Sam house in the middle of nowhere. . . .'"

The mounts are below us, down the hill. They're going through their cast-off tack. Some are so mad at the bits, they're trying to destroy them. I wonder if I can get any of that tack for myself. Well-behaved Sams like me don't ever need reins and bits, but those things do look nice, and these are silver. Maybe some would fit on my knife belt.

The mounts seem much too quiet for a batch of twenty-one Sams. They hardly talk at all, except a word or two now and then when they have to, but they pat each others' shoulders a lot. They keep looking around as if waiting to be captured and brought back and maybe poled. They haven't been free long enough to know how it feels. I guess by now I do know. *Sort of* know. Except I've never been without Little Master. And a good thing, too, or I'd be choked to death. Without him, maybe dead a lot of times.

Jane is listening to my story almost as much as Little Master is. My father comes up, and Jane says, "For heaven's sake," to him again. She's still angry about the way he threw me down. He sits near us, listening, too. And staring at me. I see on his face that he's going through about ten different feelings all in a row. He frowns, he wonders, he gives up, he doesn't give up.

Then there's a kind of giving over. That's a lot to see on somebody else's face, especially a face like my father's, but I know it's something like all that.

Before I finish telling about the three Wild Sams who live in the woods, my father goes back down and sits with the guards' mounts. Maybe he already knows how it ends. After I get that baby Hoot on his feet and lost, I just tell the story in the regular way. (If my father does know the end, I wonder was it Tutu told him? I laugh out loud to think of my little-bitty father sitting on Tutu's lap. Little Master wants to know why I'm laughing so he can laugh, too, but when I tell him, he doesn't think it's funny.)

When my father sits with them, the mounts bunch up around him. A lot of them use hand signals instead of talking. My father speaks to them mostly that way. I wish I knew what they were saying.

I'd like to talk to the young ones, but I have to go on telling. Since Little Master just saved my life, I owe him at least the end of the story.

I'll bet those three young mounts can talk just fine. I mean they can't have mouths utterly ruined in just a few years. And they've only just hardly grownup. I mean no one would ever make somebody my age into a guards' mount. How could somebody my age have done enough terrible things? But maybe, back when I'd just arrived . . . just been taken from my mom . . . that time when I wouldn't get up and go for my training workout. . . . If I'd kept that up, not even let them explain things to me, maybe I would have gotten to be one.

Anyway, those Sams don't want me there with Little Master

on my shoulders. I do have a good scar and they don't know I got it saving a Hoot.

Later, there's food. Every mount carried some. It's mostly dry cakes like we always have, but there's fruit and cheese and nuts. They have all the best stuff. They're supposed to be healthy because of their job. Back home, I was supposed to be healthy, too. I haven't had any of that sort of thing for months and months. They give some to my father and he brings it up to us.

I ask him about those hand signals and I tell him I like how they look. "But what were you talking about?"

"Just ta—ta—ta—ta. . . ." Long pause, then a loud, "*Talk!*" as if that was a terribly important word. (He's not ever going to tell me anything. I don't know why I asked.)

He's given Jane and Little Master and me all the food he brought. While we eat, he sits, elbows on his knees, examining his hands—turning them over and back again. I wonder what he's reading there. New scars, I suppose. I hope he's thinking how he shouldn't have used those hands to shake me so hard and throw me down.

Little Master eats fast, as though someone will take his fruit away, and all of it at the same time. Stuffs it in. He's not tasting anything. I say, "Hey," and then everything is gone. *I* take tiny bites to make it last as long as possible. I want to think about this food and remember back when I was important enough to get it (or better than this) every day.

Jane tries to give some of her fruit back to my father, but he won't take it. He lets her feed him a few orange sections and grapes, one at a time. That makes them laugh. I can't remember if I've ever seen him laugh. Smile, maybe—a little bit.

I make Little Master stay back with Jane so I can go down to those three young ones that I cut loose. They move closer to each other and away from me. The way they look at me you'd think I was older and wiser, but they have got to know a lot more, and more important, things than I do.

First I sit—not too close—and don't say anything. They don't, either. They all three have painted-on mustaches, though it looks as if two have beginnings of their own real ones. I guess not good enough yet. They don't have misshapen mouths as my father and the older mounts mostly do.

Then, finally they ask—and it's my father's question over again. "Whose side are you on?"

And then, "Are you a Wild or a Tame?"

And, "That guard that almost killed you was our captain. She's as bad as a Hoot gets."

"I know that."

"We wouldn't have put up with her here."

"I know."

They all sputter a little but nothing like my father. And even to me they use signs. They take for granted that I know them. I pretend I do.

"How did you get to be guards' mounts? What did you do?"

"We were incorrigible."

They leer. They're proud of it.

"We're worse than any Wilds."

"Still are."

They start to laugh and snarl and make gestures as if they'll leap-and-choke me, but I don't flinch. I don't like people to think I'm a Wild. They think Wilds don't know anything, which they don't. I pull my lip up and out to prove I'm not, and then I ask, "So what did you do that was so bad?"

"Revolt. Big one."

"We killed Hoots."

"All of us did."

"What about you?"

"You mean me?"

"You took a pretty good hit. Looks like maybe top-to-bottom."

I have a lot on, but my leggings are too short. You can see my calf and ankle, and my cheek and my neck down to my collarbone.

First I feel proud, and I don't know what kind of lie to tell. I should have practiced one. But I'm not on their side anyway. Only sort of, when it comes to what they wear, and how they march, banging down with their metal heels. I guess I'm on a very small side, with only Little Master and me in it. I might as well stick up for us.

I point my chin up to where Little Master is—sitting on Jane's lap now. It looks as if she's telling him a story, too. "I saved that baby Hoot," I say.

The young one—that youngest—the one I wanted most of all to be friends with. . . .

Talk about fast as a rattlesnake or the leap-and-choke. He punches me. *Two* punches. One two. Before I have time to even think one. I fall back, about as hard as when my father threw me, but this time I get up fighting. Except he's trained for it. He knows tricks and nasty punches to the wrong places. And he kicks. And he knows how to block. I don't come close to hitting him. Not even once. I don't know anything. I didn't even know there were things to know. My father never taught me. If I lose, it'll be my father's fault.

And here he is. Everybody (except me) stops when they see him. Nobody says a word. I keep hitting, but, like before, all I hit are the mount's wrists. My father grabs me.

"Go ahead, throw me down. Throw me away again."

"Never."

He keeps on holding. When I stop fighting (what's the use anyway?), it turns into a hug. He's too big and sweaty for hugging. All us Wilds smell. (It's what they call a bear hug, though I'd like to know who ever got hugged by a bear, and, if so, I'd like to know why, and did they live to tell about it?)

And he hugs too tight. He says, "I wasn't. . . . Never, never, never." His wet breath right in my ear.

He leads me back to Jane (his iron grip still). When we get up there, he *lets* me pull away. I walk back towards the mounts a little and squat to look at the cast-off tack. I pick up a bit. It's one of the best. The cheek-pieces are silver and in the shape of a leaping Sam, one leg way out front. It has a little goldish lump in the middle where your tongue goes. If you pull on the sides, I'll bet that lump turns up against the roof of your mouth.

I hide it under my vest. I can't wait to try it out—see what that lump feels like, but I don't dare until I get by myself, just me and Little Master. My father would have a worse-than-ever fit if he saw me with that in my mouth—no matter how beautiful it is. I wonder, does he care anything *at all* about art?

Back when I was going to be the mount of The-Ruler-Of-Us-All, I wonder what I would have worn. I mean, for show. Would I have gotten to have a mustache? I wonder if Little Master knows. I'll bet gold instead of silver. So now, because of my father, I'll never get to look good. I look down at myself, this sheep-yarn sweater, too-short leather leggings. I had to cut the toes out of my shoes. For sure I look like a Wild.

So far I've managed to avoid calling my father anything at all. I never needed to. I don't know what to call him. Maybe Heron. If I call him Beauty I'll bet I'd get another shaking.

I go back up and tap him on the shoulder.

"I have to know how to fight."

"*No!*"

"I *have* to."

"I want . . . you not. . . . *Not* like me."

"Don't you want me to defend myself?"

"You weren't. Not defen . . . *ding.*"

(I'm going to ask those three young ones. If one of them won't teach me, then I'll just fight with them and watch to see how they do it.)

Then my father does what he always does, turns and walks away. From everything. We're at the saddle of the mountain. There's a peak on each side of us. He turns and walks towards the highest. Like he does, he picks a steep way.

When I sit down by Jane, she says, "There he goes again. One of these days. . . . Poor old Seattle. He's going to kill himself by mistake. Or maybe on purpose." She stands up and watches until he's behind the cliffs, then she starts packing things up. "He never had a chance to be even a little bit happy. Ever."

Little Master crawls over to my lap. "*We* have," he says. "We have a lot of fun."

Jane says, "In solitary, too, sometimes. Those Hoots know what that's like. They're herd animals just like we are. They know." Hard to tell if she's talking to us or not. "Isn't it odd that solitary should make a person even more solitary?" Then she says, "I wish I knew. . . . Oh dear." And then she looks up towards where my father must be, though by now you can't see him.

Chapter Eight

My father isn't back yet. Jane doesn't know what to do with twenty-one guards' mounts. Are they in charge with Heron gone? And where will they be safest? She doesn't think they should stay here. All she knows is to take them back to the village and wait for Heron. If anybody comes after them, she can hide them up at the mountain ruins. She tells me maybe it's me they'll follow, not her. Since Heron isn't here, it's maybe only me.

"But they don't like me with Little Master on me." (They'd like me even less if they knew he was The-Future-Ruler-Of-Us-All.) "They don't like me anyway."

"You're Heron's son. You have obligations. Just like he has."

Not again. I had enough obligations when I was the mount of Little Master About-To-Be-The-Ruler. And I'm still the only one responsible for him because if *any* of us ever find out who he is, they'll kill him in a minute.

"Well, if my father's got all these obligations, where is he? Why isn't he here doing his obligations like he should be doing?"

That stops her.

"But they won't like a Sue, let alone a *Tennessee*, leading them."

(I know *exactly* how they feel.)

"Maybe if we both do it. I mean we're the only ones who know the way."

The mounts hardly know how to walk, except in rows. Up here the ground is so rough there's only a few places where they can do that. They're going to have to change. Well, I had to change in lots of ways, and I didn't want to, so I guess they can.

We dip down into a high valley and then start up again, towards the last pass before the village. It's even higher than the one where the halfway hut is—used to be. We're up beyond trees, even the ones that are blown sideways into funny shapes. We're up where the lupine is dwarfed and flattened. Everything is.

Mostly we're walking through piles of rocks. That's all there is to this mountain, but they've made a pretty good path here. The guards' mounts have to go one-by-one. Their metal heels clang, but not, anymore, in any rhythm. They're too busy watching their footing to keep track.

Jane goes first. She knows the way the best. And I come right behind her.

But what happens is what always happens up here in the mountains. (Another good reason why they shouldn't have the village way up here.) Nobody's been noticing the clouds. Or I haven't. A hail storm. We run. Any direction. Everybody. *Every* direction.

I pull Little Master off my shoulders and curl myself over him to protect him as I run. Little Master has his big hands spread over his head. I run, but there's no place to go. Except I have to go someplace fast. It's Jane pushes us down, squeezes us partly under a slightly overhanging rock and curls herself around us. These mountain hail stones aren't just any old hail stones. She's going to get herself bruised.

No wonder those plants hug the rocks and stay small.

I say, "I don't need for you to do this. I can do it."

She doesn't answer. She just hangs on to us tight.

There's thunder and lightning, too. I worry about the guards with all that metal on their feet. My father taught me to throw down any Hoot pole and anything metal I had. I worry about my father. What will we. . . . What will *everybody* do if my father doesn't come back?

The storm lasts about the usual for a hail storm. Can't be more than a few minutes, though it feels long.

After it blows on by, nobody moves. We untangle ourselves from ourselves a bit and lift our heads.

There's not a single sign of life, but everything's all scrubbed and pink and shiny, with little piles of hail here and there, in hollows, and around the edges of things.

Jane is looking around at everything. I ask her, "Are you all bruised up?"

She says, "You know, I always thought of this as mine. Even the mountains in the distance. Even places I've never been. I always had pennyroyal in my top buttonhole to smell as I walked." Then she says, "Smell. The Hoots always say they can smell the sun. I wonder if this now is how it smells."

"What about my father?"

"I hope it's as pretty as this and smells this good where he is."

We stand up. There's no sign of anybody. The light is all pinkish and luminous. Jane . . . she's already kind of pinkish, what with her hair and her freckles: Now she glows. For a minute I see her as my father must see her. For a minute being too-thin looks pretty good.

Then I see the guards' mounts getting up and wandering back to the trail. I can see even they are admiring how everything looks.

"I've spent my whole life climbing and picking flowers," Jane says. "Wind and hail or anything. Your father needs to wander around like I did. I had all, all, *all* these mountains to be free in, while he was in a paddock all his life, even as a baby."

"Well, I was, too."

"Oh, Charley, I'm so sorry." She turns from the view and tries to hug me but, just in time, I squat for Little Master to mount.

"I liked it. Lots of times I wish I was back there with my mother. You don't know anything about it."

At least she has the sense to say, "I know I don't. I was seven when I was rescued."

"You call this . . . all this right now, climbing and climbing all the time and then hail and everything, rescued?"

All she says is, "But look! Look!"

I guess I really don't know how it was for my father any more than she does, because, if his mother was Tutu, she had to be off racing or training. And when she was there, I'll bet she was all tired out. My mom was there all the time. I don't know what it would be like to not have your mom around.

We get back on the trail, Jane leading as before, but I walk with the three younger mounts. I feel funny with Little Master on me. It's scary. They could hurt him. But this is very, very important. I want to ask the one who hit me if he'll teach me how to fight.

First he says, "You're crazy," and then he says, "Why, so you can beat me up?"

"No. I promise not to."

"You couldn't anyway." He makes a sound, kind of as if spitting. I've heard that sound a few times before. Always about the Hoots. It means they're nothing, worthless. Then he clears his throat at me and does spit. All the things Merry Mary told me not to do. So did Sunrise. And I never do them.

I want to say . . . I *should* say, and for his own good, you're not supposed to do that, but no sense in getting into another fight now, when I know I'd lose. And I want to get on his good side.

"Well, will you? Will you teach me?"

The trail narrows and I have to walk behind him. Then it broadens out right where the view of the village is. For a long time we haven't been able to see the farthest mountains. We had to get over this last rise first. All of a sudden, there they are. As the mounts come around the corner, they gasp, or even shout, and stop, and the others bump into them. I remember how I felt when I first saw the valley with the snow-capped mountains behind it—far as you can see, snow-capped mountains.

I'm even impressed all over again. I almost shout myself.

Everybody spreads out and sits down to rest and look. Little Master dismounts and wobbles up on one of the rocks (all by himself!) to be even higher. The view is so good nobody talks about it. Nobody even says, "Look." It's as if it's fragile and talking would spoil it—as if they want to hang on to the feeling of the very first sight of it as long as they can.

Then I hear, right by my ear, a nasty, spitting whisper. "What do you have that'll make it worth my while?"

First I think. I don't have much except that silver bit, which I doubt he'd want. It might be his anyway. Then I start to answer that I have to think, but my voice does one of those jumpy, yodelly kind of things, and I stop right in the middle. I don't like to talk much myself these days because my voice does funny things. I wish I knew my real age. Just because my teeth looked eleven-years-old back then doesn't mean I might not be twelve or even thirteen. And that was months ago. Anyway, I guess I know a little bit about how it feels not to get your words out when you want to.

"And what about that Hoot of yours? I wouldn't mind teaching you both. Give him to me and I'll teach you anything you want."

I'm just about to have another losing fight when a runner comes up the trail from behind us. It's that same runner that I met at the pond. He remembers me right away and comes straight to me as though I was important. He sits beside me first thing and starts drinking from his canteen. But he spits out the first batch and then drinks again. Everybody gets up and gathers around us. He doesn't talk at all, just blows for a few minutes. And looks at the view. Then he tells me he found Merry Mary. And I say, "Where? Can I go there?"

But he's not running all the way up here just to give me that news, though at first I thought so. The real news is for my father. He looks around for him and forgets about me. Then he tells us that Hoot guards have locked up thousands of Sams and Sues. Some they've marched off to the East. All the towns around here are either empty or completely closed off with shock wires.

"Because of Heron," he says. He grins at me and punches me hard on the shoulder, as if this is the best news he could ever tell me. "Because of your father!"

It sounds as if it's exactly the way it used to be when they first landed and took over. Now they'll have to do it all over again. It's all our fault. Things were nicely settled down. Everybody was happy. Everybody had a job to do that suited them, Seattles for strength, Tennessees for speed, the old and lame ones cooking and cleaning and farming. . . . We all worked together. There were plenty of really, really, *really* good things to eat. How can you be even a little bit civilized without Sams and Sues keeping at their jobs like they're supposed to?

That young mount is still right beside me. "I'll bet your Hoot friends are singing their usual tunes. Kindness is the best policy—as long as it's behind the wires."

Why does he always have to lean so close and spit when he talks?

There's no point in waiting for my father here. There's nothing to do except go on to the village and wait for him. I don't see why he's so important. What does he ever *do?* Except run off whenever he feels like it, right in the middle of the most important things?

We start down into the beautiful valley. It's not so steep now, and on this side of the pass it's different: Greener, bigger trees, different kinds of flowers, lots more animals. Little things skitter away as we come. Jays squawk.

Jane knows the name of all the flowers, but all she knows are Sam and Sue names, not Hoot names. I wonder which is more sensible to try to learn? I don't want to waste time with a lot of useless words. And why does everything have to have a name, anyway? Down to the smallest piece of the smallest flower? Even ones you can hardly see?

This time I walk near the front again with Jane and the runner. I want to ask about my mother, and I want to get away from the mount, but he walks beside me. Does he want to torment us, or what? I must be a lot of fun for him. I'll bet he'd like me to pick another fight. And at first I wanted to like him the best.

I don't want to ask about my mother in front of him. It'll just prove more things about me that I'd rather he didn't know. But he heard the runner. He makes that spitting noise again, right in my ear, and says, "We don't have mothers."

I wish my father would come back.

That runner has news from all over, and he asks Jane things, too. He wants to know all about what happened here so he can tell about it to other places. He likes that there are twenty-one big Seattles willing to fight. He's going to tell that all over. He has a miniature pole and his big knife. He says, would you

believe it, these small poles are our invention? He says Hoots
don't think we were capable of inventions of this sort. He says
they're in for a surprise.

I wonder what it's like being a runner. You'd get to wear a
camouflage suit and racing shoes and a big Hoot kind of hat.
You could go everywhere and hear things and see sights. Do a
lot of good, too. Bring messages. Help people find each other.
Tell people who died. Seattles could do it.

I walk as close to him as I can, but so does the mount. He
wants to hear, too. I don't care what he thinks. I'll ask about
Merry Mary, anyway. I have a mother and I care about her and
I don't care who knows it.

"Well, what about Merry Mary?"

"Normally she could be rescued fairly easily because that's
a lax, badly-run place, but she's in a special enclosure now, right
next to the Hoot warrens. They're upset with her because she
has a new baby, but it's not a Seattle and not even a half-
Tennessee. They don't know how that happened. They suspect
she fell in love."

Love!

I stop. I go kind of numb. I don't want to hear any more
about it. I have to think. I wait till almost everybody goes by,
but that mount stays right with me. How can I think with him
around? I don't want to fight—well, I do, except not right
now—but I don't know if I can keep myself from it. Anyway,
I don't care if I get beat up or not.

He's just a little bit behind me and I start to trip—a lot of
times. My left toe keeps hitting my right heel over and over. I
finally figure out he's doing it. He just touches my left heel with

his toe . . . just enough and just at exactly the right time to push my toe into my heel. I can see how that's a good trick when you have to march in ranks all day long and get bored.

The minute he sees that I know he's doing it, he really trips me. I go down, hard. Little Master goes flying. That's rare for a Hoot. They're so fast and hold on so tight. But this time it's a good thing. He goes right into a mountain currant bush instead of down on the rocks with me.

One part of me wants to come up fighting, but the other part of me is too stunned and hurt. I have to wait a few minutes before I can even begin to get up. Some of the mounts stop beside me. Since those older ones don't talk much, they kind of tip their heads slanty-wise and raise their eyebrows. I know what they mean, which is, am I all right?

I let a couple of them help me up. They won't touch Little Master, though. One says, "Leave 'im. Starve 'im." He has almost as many scars as my father.

The young mount makes that spitting sound again. More than the sound, he spits—towards me. It hits my shoe. Then he goes on ahead with the others. Those guards' mounts don't have any manners at all.

I wait till everybody goes by and then I help Little Master out of that bush. He's not hurt except for a lot of scratches. He's so droopy—ears down by his cheeks—he's crying. We're both shaky. We sit on a rock. We're going to lag way behind on purpose. We can't get lost. Most of the time you can see where you're supposed to end up.

No wonder everybody says guards' mounts are the worst of any of us. I'm glad I behaved myself back then when I first came to Little Master, though I was disappointed that I only had a baby to be my host. That was before I knew that was the best way . . . to begin us together and train us together from the beginning.

We go on, but slowly. After a bit, Little Master says, "Your mother was *bad*."

"I know that."

"We don't love that way, so we never make love mistakes that get us into trouble."

"I don't want to talk about it."

"She should have known better."

"She did. I know she did."

But what I really know is, she didn't. She was as bad as my father. Worse. With her it wasn't even with a Tennessee, which means it has to have been with a nothing. What else is there? Doesn't she care anything at all about good strong legs? About being the best there is?

I keep having to change my mind about everything, and now even about my mother. How can you change your mind about your mother? That should be the one set-forever thing. But what if it's not her fault? She'd better have good reasons.

"She didn't know any better, or she wouldn't have done it."

"I said I don't want to talk about it. I have to think." But I'm not going to think.

"*You* wouldn't love that way, would you?"

"Of course not."

What if Merry Mary gets rescued? Then that baby will be with her.

We're way behind everybody now. Little Master is happy

about that. He rests his cheek right next to mine like he usually does. "I knew you wouldn't," he says and starts to sing. I punch out at nothing as we walk: One, two; one, two. Really fast. I need to practice.

All of a sudden Little Master says, "Stop! Listen!"

I stop.

"Duck us down behind these rocks. Quickly, quickly. Duck!"

Then I hear it, too. It sounds like a thunderstorm, and what good is ducking? But I trust Little Master to know more than I do. Then I see it. A great cloud of dust coming down the mountain. I make sure Little Master has his head behind where mine is.

I always think of the boulders on the trail as having come down a long time ago, but here they come now, though mostly small stuff, right over us, bouncing stones, some big, but mostly gravel and sand. We can't breathe. We're inside dust. If we'd been walking any faster, we'd have been away from this big boulder we're behind, and we'd be dead.

When it starts to die down—which takes a long time—we look out and up, pebbles still bouncing down on us and so much dust we can't see—it's in our nose, in our teeth. . . . But then there's a shadow shape. Big and dark. Sliding down in a swirl of dust. It stops and stands, right in the middle of the trail. It's still too dusty to see very well, but it's got to be a bear. It's too big for anything else.

. . . Except . . . it's my father—rode the avalanche down. Like it was a mount. He must have. Like a big avalanche god. Jane said these mountains all seemed to belong to her, but I don't think so. Maybe my father didn't grow up with any of it, but it belongs to him. He doesn't ever look right, except next to a mountain or a pile of rocks. He must have started this slide in the first place and then rode it down.

He turns and sees us. There's a light breeze and the dust is blowing off, down the trail behind him. He's looking at us just the way I must be looking at him. Like: Where did *you* come from?

"Charley!"

Then, "What are you doing here? Are you all right?" (He's so upset he can talk pretty much perfectly.) And then, "You're all right." He says that three times.

We just stand there. We don't know what to do, even my father. Then Little Master gives me a kick as if to remind me: *Do* something. He seldom has to kick me, usually just squeezes a bit. Even so, I'm used to moving forward when he does it. I move to my father. He grabs me.

"Charley!"

And there I am, flat up against all that dust and grit and gravel and smelly sweat.

"Charley!"

Stuck right into his hairy chest, practically under his arm, my cheek . . . my ear . . . as if grinding into sandpaper. I'm going to suffocate. I start to pull away, but then I see he's crying. It's kind of hard to tell for sure. First I think it's his sweat dripping down on me, but then I know it's not, and he's breathing in a shaky way.

I don't know what to do. I don't like it. I don't want a grownup to cry, and I don't want somebody that big and strong to do it. But I stay there anyway. I can't move. I feel all stiff and kind of stuck. It's as if my mind wants me to get away fast, but my body won't go.

He hangs on to me for a lot too long. All through it I'm waiting and waiting. . . . Finally he lets me go, turns away, and doesn't look at me. I guess he embarrassed himself. Or maybe he can see how I wish he hadn't done that.

For sure those were tears. I see the clean spots on his cheeks.

We all three sit on the same rock Little Master and I hid behind. My father takes out his canteen and gives us each a drink. Then he wipes our faces. He doesn't bother with his own and he doesn't drink but one sip. Then we just sit and breathe for a while . . . spit out dust . . . pick it from the corners of our eyes. . . .

I glance at him and I see even worse than Wild and uncivilized. Except even Little Master looks Wild, which Hoots never do. Who ever heard of a Wild Hoot? But I can't stop thinking how my father came down in that cloud of dust, rode the avalanche, and how some day I could do that, too.

We start back towards the village, but it's a lot slower than before, what with all this landslide in the way. We have to climb down over the debris. Some of those rocks are huge, but most are small. We struggle along behind my father. He's not going very fast himself, but faster than we are. Little Master doesn't sing. He can see what a hard time I'm having, so he tries to help me with balancing. He says, "Tell him to slow down," but I say, "No!"

We go on and on without any rests at all. I think my father

forgot about us. I'm slipping and sliding and going as fast as I can. It's even worse than straight up. It starts getting to be twilight and he hasn't stopped yet. Little Master says, "Tell him you need a rest." He's looking out for his mount just as he should. But I say, "No!"

"I will then."

"*No!*"

He'd better not.

When we finally do stop, I'm too tired even to eat. There's no place to flop down, but I do anyway. Little Master climbs off and sits on my chest so as to be off the rocks. I'm lying on rocks the size of shoes, which are exactly the kind Little Master hates to sit on the most. I don't like them, either.

My father starts to get food out, but I must have fallen asleep. I don't remember anything except seeing him leaning over his pack. I'm half in a dream already. I think how I don't believe in him any more than in ghosts or fairy tales. Hoots don't believe in either one. Hoots say only primates think things like that. But my father is ghostly, right in front of me . . . a ghostly giant covered in gray dust . . . god of the mountain. When he says, slide, there's a landslide. If lightning, my father must have said, lightning. If thunder, my father said, thunder.

Chapter Nine

When I wake, it's night. At least there's moonlight. I hurt all over from lying on these rocks. I'll bet I have bruises from it.

I guess I must have been making noises, because my father is leaning over me. He's a big shadow-shape blocking out the moon. He's shaking my shoulder. "It's all right," he says. "Wake up. It's all . . . all. . . ." When he sees I'm awake, he changes from shaking me to patting. I start to sit up, but I'm too stiff, and I lie back down and make another noise by mistake. Which makes my father pat me all the more. There's something under my head and something is tucked in partly over me. I don't know what's under my head, but over me it feels like his knitted vest. Jane sure knits a lot of vests.

My father brings his canteen, lifts my head, and helps me drink. All of a sudden I worry about what happened to Little Master. Last I knew he was sitting on my chest. What did my father do with him? Then I see the moonlight glistening on his eyes not far from us. They glow so much it almost seems you could light your way with them, though of course you couldn't. But no wonder Hoots can see in the dark. He's watching us from above, but he crawls down when he sees me looking at him.

I say to my father, "But you didn't wake me."

"You needed. . . ."

I guess I did if I fell asleep before I knew it, right in the middle of him telling me things.

He says, "Sorry."

What's he sorry about now? That he let me sleep? I won't ask. He'll just try to tell me and I don't feel like waiting for him to struggle it out.

He helps me up. The moonlight is so bright you can almost see colors. You can't, but you think you can. We're past the landslide and back on the trail. And in this moonlight it's not so hard to go on. If there's anything along the trail that looks to Little Master like I need to know about it, he'll tell me.

I ask Little Master, did he sleep?

"I got bored. Everybody was asleep."

"Didn't you sleep at all?"

"Well, a little bit, but we see at night, you know—you know that, and we love full moons. There were lots of moons where we come from. They told me never less than three in the sky at a time. I went up a little bit to see the view, all shiny, just as if back where we come from."

"You never, ever, even once saw where you Hoots come from." But then I think a minute, and then I say, "You know what? Something's happening to you. You're getting yourself around. Other Hoots never do that, climb up there on rocks,

CAROL EMSHWILLER

not even a little bit. I wonder how far you can go?"

He doesn't answer, just moves his cheek from mine and puts his chin on top of my head instead. He's thinking.

My father trots along ahead of us at a nice, Seattle, long-distance pace. He'd probably be going faster if it wasn't for me.

Little Master says, "You're right, I am." But it's so much later I have to think back to remember what he's talking about.

We pass another good view place, almost as good in the moonlight as it was in daytime. There's fires down there in the village. Like signals just for us. At the edge of town there's this homey glow in three places, as if one fire for each of us, even Little Master. You can hardly see the houses in this moonlight, they're too much the same color as the rocks they're on. Those fires almost makes me happy to be going back. Well, I am: There's food and rest and warmth, and I'll be glad to see Sunrise. She'll be glad to see me, too.

I'll bet they heard the rockslide, maybe even all the way down there. I'll bet they wonder if we're all right.

I wish we were coming back with my mom's picture and Little Master's doll. We never even thought to get them with those guards' mounts around. We probably even left some food up there. If I had her picture, I'd hang it in our lean-to. It would make it look civilized. Especially it would if I could have had that silver frame. My father made me a bookcase, but it's not even half the size of the one I had in my stall, and there's only four books that really belong to me. (I suppose it's not democratic to keep a book all to yourself, even the ones you own.) The walls are just rocks and the window is tiny. "Because of the cold," my father said. The walls are thick, so

140

you have to get right up to the window to see out. All it looks out on are mountains, no fountains, no walkways, no avenues, and no big trees. . . . Vegetables grow right up next to the houses.

I'd put my mother's picture across from our cot, I guess, even after what she's done. She's beautiful, her hair tied up on top in a fancy hairdo. You don't see that at the village. I hope she has a good excuse for falling in love. I wonder if we'll have to rescue the baby, too. I'd be ashamed to have a brother or sister that's not a Seattle. I'd even be ashamed to have it up here where there's hardly a decent Seattle for miles around but me and my father. Up here they hardly know what a good one looks like.

At dawn we stop to eat dry cakes and watch the color come to the mountain tops, our backs to the sun. My father is the most sunrise-watching person I ever met.

We sit, and pretty soon I'm telling my father about my mother and her new baby. I don't do it to make him feel bad, I do it to see if maybe he can say something that will help me understand things a little bit better.

"No dif . . . ferent from me and Jane," he says.

"But at least she's a Tennessee. What if this is with a complete, absolute nothing?"

"There is no nothing."

"But what if it's somebody who can't trot at all?"

He shakes his head—so many times I should have counted, but I didn't start in time. Then he blows out like that runner did. "Someday you'll love," he says.

"*I* won't. That's wrong."

"Human." He shakes his head again.

When we get up to go on, he stops me and takes off the belt he gave me. At first I think he's taking it back, maybe because of what I said about the nothings, but then he takes the knife and makes another hole. I'm getting thinner. It felt like it. I've been hungry ever since I left our Hoot home and especially in these last few days. But I hope I'm getting taller, too. Sunrise would know. She keeps track.

My father takes out an apple he must have been saving since the mounts brought out all that fresh food. It's bruised and dusty and wilted. "Share. You . . . with . . . him," he says. It's such a mess, if I wasn't so hungry I wouldn't even look at it, but I take the knife and cut it in half. Little Master makes a sneery face, but I guess he's hungry, too. He gobbles it as fast as he did that fruit before. Hoots can do that. He only takes two bites. Two of his baby teeth come out as he does it. My voice is changing, and his teeth are falling out. I liked him better with his little white baby teeth. Those big, grownup yellow ones always bothered me. Besides, they make me think of trainers—and creatures (Hoots do it too) that smile big smiles just to show how dangerous they are.

I wonder about my father. Back there all he got was a few grapes. I say, "*You* don't eat." (I don't ask it until I finish the apple. I'm really, really hungry. I can hardly stand it.)

"I do. Some. But I'm not growing. I remember . . . how it felt . . . when I . . . at your age."

Then he starts to give a speech. It's so hard to keep track of what he's saying. And here's another "sorry" or three.

"I didn't . . . mean for you. . . ." And then he waves at the rockslide debris behind us. "I thought you . . . were . . . gone by. . . . Safe."

"It's all right. We are safe."

This time I'm the one who gets up. I squat for Little Master to mount and then start trotting down the trail. I go at a fast pace. My father will see how strong I am. He'll watch my legs. He'll think how it's worthwhile being a pure Seattle. He'll think how a nothing really *is* worth nothing.

Though we can see the village, it takes us most of the rest of the day to get down. Sunrise and Jane and a couple of young nothings (they sure look like nothing to me) come up to meet us. They bring us goat's milk and cheese and squash cake. We all sit and eat even though we'll be down soon. Those young ones look at my father like he's special. And they even look at me like that. Well, compared to them we are. Well, compared to *any*body we are. Those two nothings whisper to each other. I can tell they're whispering about me because they keep glancing at me. I keep my leg muscles tightened up so they'll see what legs are supposed to look like.

Dirty as my father is, Jane hugs him first thing. I don't like to watch that hugging sort of thing. Even if you turn away fast, you can't miss the way her hand rubs up and down on the back of his neck, which I'm sure is all sweaty. Then she hugs me. So does Sunrise. Usually Sunrise knows better.

Even as Jane hugs him, my father asks about the guards' mounts.

"We put up some tents next to the mess hall. Those men are odd. They fight among themselves a lot and hardly ever talk."

"Like me."

"Not at all like you."

We sit and eat. This odd food is beginning to taste good. Or I'm so hungry I like anything. Right now it's as if nothing ever tasted better. I know it isn't as scientifically made for us Sams and Sues as our dry cakes. It can't be. Dry cakes may not taste so good, but they were made especially for us, and we can last forever on them. Hoots say taste doesn't matter, anyway, but I've noticed Little Master cares about it, too. Of course he's still young. He doesn't know any better. And being with us is spoiling him, just like being with these Wilds is spoiling me.

When we get back to the village, we have another supper and then collapse. Little Master curls up with me, and Sunrise piles a big fluffy quilt over us. That night there's one of those mountain storms, but I'm so tired I only wake up enough to know it's happening. Normally I'd be at the window in two seconds, Little Master, too, but now we can't stay awake to appreciate it. Once, in a thunderstorm, right from this window, I saw a fireball roll down the mountain. I wouldn't mind seeing that again.

We don't wake up till most of the way through the next day, when Sunrise brings us breakfast in bed.

"You'll never sleep tonight if you don't get up pretty soon." She pats us both even though everybody knows you're not supposed to pat Hoots.

I finally get almost enough to eat.

After, there's something special I want to do. I sneak us into the hills behind the village. That's easy. Our hut is on the edge of things, and there's a deep ditch just behind it where the water runs off when the snow melts. Now it's dry and full of jackrabbits. There's a fox lives around there, too. (I've seen the fox and a rabbit just sit there together as if they were friends, which makes sense since those jackrabbits are just as big as the fox.)

We drop down into the ditch, trot along it, and come out after we get around the corner. We came here to hide sometimes. I know it really isn't a secret place. They probably knew where we were, but they let us be. None of the other children wanted to come when we were here, or even when we weren't. Probably having a Hoot here contaminated it. Or maybe it was me. I never wanted to be with them, either. I'd rather be with those mounts, even if it means fighting. At least they're all Seattles.

First I find my secret piece of mirror. Then I feel around my lip where a mustache should be. I do feel something there, and I do see a little bit of fuzz.

But that's not why I came out here. I want to find out just how far Little Master can walk. And I want it to be a secret.

First I feel his legs. Not that I don't feel them around my neck all the time, but that's different. I can tell they're a lot better than they used to be. Then I set him off walking, first slightly downhill, but then back up, and down and up again. He can go pretty far. He says he could go farther if he had to. I say he can go even farther if we work on it, and I say too bad we don't have a go-round.

I work him like our old trainer did. I yell the same yells, "Do! Do it! Do it!" He tells me to stop yelling and not to forget he's The-Future-Ruler-Of-Us-All. I say, "This is how you Hoots always do. They yelled at us all the time. *They* didn't care who you were."

"But a Sam should never do that to a Hoot. Especially not to *me*."

"Well, I'm the Seattle of The-Future-Ruler-Of-Us-All. Remember how you picked me out from the four best? Us four weren't just anybody. We were already picked out from thousands."

"Hoots are better than the best of *any* of you."

"They're not."

"Are! Are, are! You know they are." He crouches on those stronger legs of his as if for the leap-and-choke.

Leap-and-choke! Hasn't he learned *anything*?

"Haven't you learned anything?"

All sorts of thoughts go through my head in about half a second. How he can walk farther now, maybe all the way back to the village. How he could leap twice as far on those legs and grab me, even though I'm more than two yards away. Maybe now it's the run-and-leap-and-choke.

"Do you really want to do this to the one-and-only mount of all the mounts around here that will accept you and that you've learned to communicate with by the slightest, *slightest*, *tiniest* pressure? The mount that knows what you mean every time you wiggle? You don't know any other life than with me." (Of course the opposite is true, too.) "Think, for heaven's sake! Do you ever think?"

I guess I got through to him, because his ears collapse, clunk, completely down on each side of those absolutely huge eyes, which always look watery, but now more than ever.

"Besides, around here in the wild with the Wilds, *I'm* the one in charge." But I say that in a nice way.

"Don't tell and tell and tell me like you did. You were being exactly like a trainer."

"I was. On purpose. I promise I won't do that anymore. But you promised things before, crossed your heart you wouldn't even *look* like you'd choke me. You have to promise that over again."

Then I see how his feet are bloody. Now I'm thinking, don't *I* know anything! Don't *I* have my eyes open! I'm the one that should be crossing my heart and being sorry.

"I'm stupid," I say. "Stupid, stupid, and *you're* the smart one. Why didn't you say?"

"I was trying to be a good Future-Ruler-Of-Us-All."

"I guess you proved that."

I squat and he mounts. He hangs on tight, his cheek tight up next to mine, and I trot him back.

I'm thinking to wash him and bandage him up, but when we come back there's a meeting going on. There's mounts all over the place sitting on the ground and on rocks. My father and the runner are there. Everybody is. The runner is telling about other Wilds who will join with us and which Hoot towns are sealed off and have lots of prisoners.

When Little Master and I climb up from the ditch, we're practically right in the middle of it. I sit down at the top of the bank. Little Master crouches behind me, sort of piggy-back, so as not to be too noticeable.

They talk about breaking through the white lines and letting all us prisoners out. They talk about where to go first. They're going to vote.

The Wild Sams and Sues up here in the village all believe the same thing, and all the mounts believe a different thing. Which proves a lot about democracy. What's the sense of any of it, if all the Wilds agree and there are only twenty-one mounts? The mounts will lose every single time.

Then my father gives a speech. Except of course he can't *give* it, but it's his. He wrote it out last night in the middle of the night instead of sleeping, and Jane is supposed to give it for him. She starts to. Except she's nervous. All those mounts scare her.

"The Hoots are here to stay," she says. I can hardly hear her. "They've no way of going back where they came from. They'll need some kind of transport that isn't us. Do you think they'd have to ride around on us if they had the machinery not to do it?"

Jane is terrible. I've heard enough speeches back when there were contests in the arena and the Hoots would talk about the races in their big, resonating, ho, hoing voices. I could never do that, but my voice is better than Jane's. It may yodel when I don't want it to, but it's loud, and it means what it says. And I'm not afraid of mounts, even though they knocked me down and spit at me and tripped me.

I put Little Master down, go right out, and push Jane away and grab the paper from her. I start over from the beginning.

"The Hoots are here to stay."

When *I* say it, good and loud, the mounts yell and boo and wave their fists like punching the air. It's that same one-two, one-two. All the mounts do it.

I say, "They've no way of going back where they came from."

"Kill them. So kill them."

Mounts all yell it, but Wilds don't.

That's when my father jumps up yelling, "No," a whole row of nos.

Then Little Master. . . . I can't believe it. He walks right down in front by himself and gives a Hoot ho. Not as big as he could, but big enough. One is all it takes. All it ever takes. Except this time I think they would have stopped, just seeing a Hoot walk.

For a minute everybody's too surprised to do anything, but then they get their wits back, and they—the mounts, not the Wilds—jump towards Little Master and towards me. My father hits the ones in front. Two go flying, right into the ones behind them. Then he kicks the one coming in from the side. He's shouting his nos again.

I just stand there watching. By the time I think to try to help my father and fight, too, they've stopped.

Yes! I *must* . . . I must . . . learn to fight!

Then there's gasps—everybody—dozens of gasps all at the same time.

When my father and I turn around, there's one mount dead, blood all over his fancy mustache. Nobody could have done it except Little Master. I suppose to save himself. I hope that was it. Well, it *was*. That mount must have tried to grab him. Don't they know any better? Or did they think because he's just a young one?

Everybody stands there. Even the mounts look shocked. Nobody moves. It's Sunrise—comes to check on the dead mount first—of course Sunrise. Then two women and a man carry him into the main lodge. Sunrise goes with them.

Was all this my fault? I mean, because I made the speech better?

Then my father gets up on the roof of the overhang, above all of us. Climbs up the rocks of the walls as if they were the cliffs. His voice is big as mine was, and clear and smooth. He's like me: When we talk, people hear it. But how come he can speak clearly sometimes, but mostly not? It's as if it has to be a life-and-death matter.

"To kill, one by one, solves nothing. We *will* make trouble, but not like this, and only where it counts. We'll kill as a strategy, to prove we won't live as they've made us live. *And* we'll find a way for them to get themselves around that doesn't involve us. We used to have Ultralites. We had scooters. We had motorized chairs. We can invent such things over again."

Can we? Can we really?

But now he's pointing at Little Master and me. "We're going to need this young Hoot. You must protect him. He's going to help us."

Well, he never asked Little Master if he wanted to help. Of course I'm not sure about myself, either. We'll wait and see what happens. Besides, not many except my father know who Little Master really is. Hoots always seem to know right away. They just look and they know, as if there's some mark we can't see, or maybe some overtones in his voice. I'm not going to tell. We'll just go along and see what happens when the Hoots see who we have here. No matter what my father thinks will happen, it probably won't. The minute the Hoots recognize their one-and-only Excellent Excellency, Future-Ruler-Of-Us-All, who knows what they'll do?

Chapter Ten

$\mathcal{B}y$ _now_ we must be hundreds of miles from where we usually always are. We're camped on a wide plain. It was full of flowers, but they're all squashed down. There's red and yellow torn bits of color tramped into the hard-packed sand. One batch of us is camped where it's salty. There's a patch of orange mold over there. That's where there used to be a lake, but now there's just a crust of silica and fungus. Hoots didn't take that water, it's been gone since way before they came. Little Master and I would like to go over there and see it up close. We'd like to wander all over but they won't let us. We have to be guarded. We're special. We're a little bit scared for ourselves, too. I told Little Master I'll defend him to the death, and he says he'll do the same for me. "Cross hearts," he says. "Cross them six times six."

"You don't even know what that is."

I guess he will now. I see him counting on his fingers and looking puzzled. I know he thinks he hasn't been learning the things The-Future-Ruler-Of-Us-All should know. Sunrise taught me all that stuff a long time ago.

We're working on ourselves in a different way—for safety's sake. He practices walking whenever he can and I practice fighting. To keep it secret, we have to do it in the tent. Except what I need is to fight *with* somebody. My father won't help. You'd think a former mount of the guards would want me to know how.

They've already rescued Merry Mary and her nobody baby. It was easy even though they had less than half the Sams and Sues we have now. I haven't seen her yet, and I'm not sure I want to, but I didn't dare tell my father that. They're going to take her up to the village. I guess I'll have to see her sometime. He thinks I still care about her. She's a big disappointment. Why did she do something like that, especially after she'd had me?

The funny thing is, she named the baby for me. Both its names! And even though it's a girl! I mean, its Hoot name is Smiley and its person name is Charlotte. And—I can't believe it, but I guess I have to—my father says she calls her Charley for short. Does she think that will make it a somebody? When my father told me, I didn't have my wits about me. I couldn't say a word. I didn't even ask why.

Here it's Sams and Sues as far as you can see. You can't see the end of us or the beginning. (Just like those little red flowers.) And every single one of us, no matter that my father keeps saying and saying otherwise, is here to get rid of Hoots. There's freed guards' mounts, and civilized Sams and Sues rescued from their stalls, but mostly it's Wilds from the mountains. You can always tell them by their homemade clothes and their hair.

They don't have hairdos at all. They just cut it short and let it lie whichever way it falls.

Little Master is the absolutely only Hoot around. Our guards' mounts keep near us all the time to guard him. I guess me, too. The mounts don't fight among themselves so much when they have a job to do. And they're glad of a job where the boss isn't a Hoot and there's nothing in their mouths. I still have that fancy bit with the chains on the sides. (They call that thing in the middle a spade.) I was worried when my father found it in the lean-to, but he said—even though it makes him throw up to look at it, I can tell—he said to bring it along and keep it handy.

There's something I never thought of before. I don't know why I didn't, because you'd think I would have, if I had any sense at all. That is, that there's a *Present*-Ruler-Of-Us-All, a grand (as they say) "Magnanimous, Munificent Excellent Excellency Ruler-Of-Us-All." All of us are saving me and Little Master for when we meet him . . . or maybe it's a her. We never can tell what sex they are, so maybe we'll never know, and anyway it doesn't ever seem to matter to them.

They say the Hoots, when they first came, caught us by surprise. They say *they* were surprised, too. First, that they were here at all, crashed, and, second, that *we* were here. They didn't know what to do with us. They didn't know if we were trainable or not. It took a long time to get where we are now. Now it's all coming undone.

There were swarms of them then, all bunched together and sparking their poles. Their spaceship was two miles long, and, since Hoots are small, it held a lot of them. Some little ones were snoozing inside their mothers. They swarmed out (of the ship and of their mothers) and jumped on us right away. Odd things happened. A strange virus got a lot of us. Their sounds could drive us crazy. Sounds could even kill. The Hoots say they didn't know that then, or they never would have sung those sounds, but some of us think they did know it.

Those poles were part of their ship's drive. They've lasted a long time but they won't last forever. Recently we found a big pile that had given out.

They always say they never killed—neither us nor our dogs—but they set a lot of fires, and they must have done *something*—must have found a way for things to happen, accidents and diseases and a lot of dangerous mistakes.

But us Wild ones have come back, breeding ourselves secretly in the mountains. My father says they can't have any idea how many of us we are. He says they lost track of us because they don't like hills, let alone mountains. They need flat and smooth places.

But we like flat places, too. Some of us here have bicycles. I had heard of them, but I never saw any until now. There's lots. Some of those bicycles have motors. Little Master likes the look of those. I like them, too. They keep saying we have a secret weapon. I wonder if those are it.

But then other things come by . . . in the sky. There's this sound above us. Little Master and I and everybody look up. There are fliers. Like the bicycles with motors and with wings. They have a Sam or Sue driving them, waving down at us.

Little Master yells. "Oh, oh, oh, yes! Yes!" He reaches up with both hands as he does when reaching for me to take him.

The day after those fliers come by . . . (We tried to count them. I say thirty-five and Little Master says thirty-eight.) . . . my father calls me and Little Master to a special secret tent. Jane has to lead us there. I don't know how she knows which one. They all look the same to me. Here my father isn't the only person in charge. There are six Sams and two Sues. Some of them aren't even Seattles. Only three Sams and the two Sues can speak properly. They all have scars, some quite nicely painted over. Not a single one of them has a decent hairdo or decent shoes, even the ones who are clearly Tame.

It's an old scarred Sue who speaks to us, not my father. She looks at us really hard, but I can tell that not even she can see who Little Master really is, and I don't think my father told anybody.

"We're sending you in by yourselves. You'll be in no danger. The Hoots have no malice. And they're partial to young things. Who ever heard of a Hoot being cruel just for the sake of it? You won't need a weapon. It's safer if you don't have one."

So I get to have the bit in my mouth in a real way, the two little etched pictures of leaping Sams at my cheeks, and silver chains hanging down on each side, and shiny black reins.

We practice first. With Little Master pulling on the reins, the bit doesn't feel so good. Every time that spade turns up against the roof of my mouth, it hurts, and it kind of gags me. I'm worried maybe I won't be able to talk so well myself pretty soon. I try to explain that it hurts, but the only way I can get him to understand is to have him put it in his mouth and me pull on it. It doesn't fit on him very well, but after that, he knows. Except he's not used to reins, so when we change back, he can't help hurting me lots of times anyway.

My father frowns and winces when he looks at me with that bit. He leans over with his hand on his forehead a lot, covers his eyes a lot, too, but then he gives Little Master a lesson. He acts like a trainer, tries to get him not to put his weight on the reins at all. He doesn't yell, though. Just whispers. "Loose elbows. . . . Loose. Loose." And to me, "Keep the back of your tongue high." But I don't think either of us is going to get good at this for a long time. I hope there's not going to be any long time about it. I'm going to have scars in and around my mouth. I guess it doesn't matter since I already have that long one all across my body, top-to-bottom. When this is over, I'll bet I'll have as many as my father. Mostly, though, I hope I can talk.

Chapter Eleven

$It's \ a$ long way. We start before dawn and expect to go till night. But the road is straight and exactly made for us long-distance runners.

We head off, just the two of us trotting along. It's like old times. I like everything about it. I haven't felt so good since I got rescued. I like the breeze, the sound of my feet crunch-crunching on the road. I like my new boots, and silk against my chest. I could keep going forever. Especially if there was a nice stall and good food waiting for me after, and Little Master giving me pats on my shoulder before climbing down, and after, too.

I tell Little Master how it feels to move along like this, legs pumping. Maybe he couldn't do it as I do, but he could do some. I know he hasn't ever felt this kind of good, but he says he thinks it feels even better up where he is.

Out of the corners of my eyes I can see the tips of his ears moving back-and-forth. He pats me more than I want to be patted. He sings: "Oh, trot me, trot me, say me. . . . Tell me all the things there are to tell. Oh, go, go, *go.*" That last go goes up so high I can't hear it. It's just a vibration. "But go," he says, "just don't you sing."

"I *know.*"

I'm feeling for my mustache, and it's there. Coming along.

We don't have anything that looks at all Wild on us, so we no longer have our knitted vests. I have pieces of the harnesses from the guards' mounts. I was glad to exchange my leggings for red shorts. There's no brush on the roads, anyway. Besides, it's hotter down here on the plains. We have a heavy canteen. I'm loaded like a Seattle usually is. I don't mind. It shows how strong I am. I'm a little thin for a Seattle but I know I look pretty good. I trot like our trainer always said to, chest out, chin in. Everything about me is just exactly right.

Little Master is wearing his best whites. We hid the new ones back there in the cliffs with his doll and Merry Mary's picture and picked them up on the way down. With the sun on him, he glitters. I do, too, what with all this silk and silver. I have black guards' mount's boots and thin, black, guards' mount's gloves. I don't care if we ever get anywhere, I'd like to keep going just like this, and dressed like this, forever, except with maybe a little bit more of a mustache.

Not long ago my father asked me what I wanted out of life. I'd never thought beyond a couple of years at the most. I always only think about how to be a good mount to The-Future-Ruler-Of-Us-All. I thought it would do my father good to hear the moral thing, so I told him that. Then my father asked, what did it mean to be a human being? I wasn't sure that was a proper question, but I went along with it and said I didn't know. He didn't tell me. How am I supposed to know if nobody tells me? It's just like six times six and dinosaurs. You don't go and discover those kinds of things for yourself. Somebody has to start you off in the right direction. I wonder if Little Master knows the answer to being human. But he's been away from his Hoot lessons a long time. He and I mostly only know the same things now.

And then there's the other question: Do I *need* to know what it means to be a human being? Actually, when it comes down to what's practical, I'd rather know how to fight.

What I think about doesn't have much to do with any of the things my father was asking. I guess most of all I want to do something really, really hard. Back home I always wanted to rescue Little Master and have our trainer see me do it. (I did get myself poled saving him, except nobody important was there to see it.) I wanted to do whatever it takes to make things go back the way they used to be, all comfortable, but they aren't ever going to be back that way, what with things like those fliers and bicycles and all those crowds of us primates milling about. And all the good stuff has probably been done already, but not by me. I hope this will turn out to be really hard. Some of it, anyway.

But right now this trotting along is the best thing I've done in months and months. Why didn't my father ask what was I *born* for instead of all those other questions, because I know this, right now, is it.

By evening Little Master is still singing and humming off and on. I can tell by what I see of his ears that he's looking all around. But then his ears prick forward and stay that way. All this time he's kept the reins hanging slack, but now he picks them up and holds them one-handed, low, and at the proper angle and the proper tension. His cheek isn't next to mine and his chin isn't on my head, so I know he's sitting up straight.

"What is it?"

"Them."

Pretty soon I hear them myself, and I see the dust they're making blow up and out towards the west. When we get closer, I see their Sams are like the guards' mounts, only dressed in blue and gold, not red and silver, no mustaches but a little black beard mark in the middle of the chin. That looks good, too.

When we get close to the first ones, they stop and line up on each side of the road and wait. Little Master gives me a squeeze, I pick up speed and we trot down the whole line.

Just as I thought, all the Hoots know who Little Master is right away. They make an odd kind of cooing sound I've never heard them make before. It's the opposite of their ho. Instead of making you feel jittery and as if you can't think or even stand it for one second more, now you feel warm and loving and loveable.

"Tell, oh tell," they say. All of them say it. They turn their heads sideways so as to look at Little Master straight on, with just one eye, and their ears go at attention, straight up. "And tell. Another time and way. Has it come? Has it come to this?"

I think to speak, but it's not me they're asking. I'm just the mount. A little pressure on the bit is all it takes to remind me to keep quiet.

"It has come," Little Master says.

I admire his dignity. He's stepped right in and taken over exactly the part he's supposed to play. When did he grow up? When did he learn all this? Or did he remember from before? Except I never saw any of this back when we were training together. He was always as much a child as I was. Even more.

They follow us into the town. First past masses of white wires. This is the biggest town I've ever seen. Little Master, too. His ears are swiveling all around. They take us past their fountain and their pond. In the center of it, as usual, the statue of a Seattle, one of the best I've ever seen. Of course he looks exactly like my father. (The best ones always do.) The mount is right in the middle of a leap. (I like that kind of action-statue the best.) The mounted Hoot raises both his arms, fingers spread, but not the thumb, because, as they say, of the four corners of the world. The Seattle holds him by his knees to keep him from falling off. I've done that for Little Master during leaps, lots of times.

There's nobody in the town but Hoots, all rolling around on stools. It looks like the only mounts here are those that came out to meet us.

I know . . . I just *know* it's because the Sams and Sues are all in prison, like they said it was when they rescued Merry Mary. Only these are let out because they needed them. And they all have bits and reins and are held in tight.

Everybody, the guards and Little Master, too, has to dismount, and we're led into a burrow with a long, long entrance way. I'm the only mount that comes along, and that's because Little

Master said so. Here's another test, crawling down the entrance way. I never did like how it felt inside a burrow, especially the entrance, but this is the worst. Who but a Hoot could stand it? When I wanted to do hard things, this isn't what I had in mind. I would much rather cause a landslide.

Little Master walks . . . walks and not wobbling . . . down the hall in front of me. (My father found him a pair of red, human-being baby shoes. Till now nobody ever did see a Hoot with shoes.) They brought him a stool just his size, but he refused it and walked in by himself. He even has his chin in and his chest out just like me—not when I'm crawling down a burrow, though.

The entrance way finally opens out to a wide room. It's even bigger than the dining lodge up at the village. Wider, that is, but not as tall. When I stand up, my head touches the ceiling. There's a batch of guards in hats. They're in a half-circle around one special Hoot. That's got to be him, The Munificent, Magnanimous Master, The-Present-Ruler-Of-Us-All.

He isn't wearing anything special. I guess you're supposed to be able to tell like they always can when they see Little Master. He doesn't have any kind of hat nor even any hairdo. Just nice whites. It's a lot like democracy.

He says, "Dear child . . . of the seven. I bare my neck." And he leans his head back, inviting the leap-and-choke. "How should we do? Say or sing it. Do. And let me see your neck."

But Little Master says, "No." Just plain no.

"Then it will have to be as it seems to be."

Little Master says just plain, "Yes."

I can't believe how dignified he is, and sure of himself.

Then he and The-Present-Ruler-Of-Us-All leave the big room. Just the two of them. Little Master doesn't even look back at me. He keeps his ears stiff—at attention. They go into a cubby at the far end of the hall. I'm glad I'm not supposed to go in there with them. As it is, I'm having a hard time even though it's a wide room. When Little Master was here, I didn't notice how short of breath I was starting to be, but now I do. I'm worried about him, but I'm beginning to worry about myself more. I don't care how elegant it is, and it is, and I don't care how many portraits of us line the walls, and they do, and in silver frames, every single one of them. I don't care about the plant stands and the plants or the soft white rugs. I shut my eyes and try to pretend I'm outside with a big blue sky above me, but even with my eyes shut I feel worse and worse. I start to shake and sweat, and my fingers feel stiff. I think I'm going to throw up, but that scares me all the more.

Maybe they can tell . . . or smell. . . . Anyway, they finally let me crawl out . . . *make* me . . . two guards prod me from behind with a pole set on low as if they don't know I can't wait to get out of there. I didn't say a word. I was willing to stay . . . sort of willing, if I had to. I knew this was one of the really hard things I needed to do, only this kind of hard thing isn't like the others. It's as if your body just won't do it even if your brains want it to. Your body would rather throw up. As soon as I'm out of there, I do.

I don't have much of a chance to catch my breath outside in the nice fresh air—I'm breathing these big, gaspy breaths—

when they put a dog collar around my neck (pretty tight, too) and lead me off, past another batch of white wires, to a big building practically all made of white wires. They sizzle and spit as we go in, even though we don't touch them. I guess this is what a prison is. I did wonder.

Before they shut me in, they take off my boots and check my feet for Wild feet, which would have big calluses and ground-in dirt, but my feet are soft and clean.

I know how to be Tame and well brought up. I don't say a single word all through it. They check my mouth tattoo. They don't have any expression on their faces, but how could they not be pleased—about my tattoo and everything else about me? When they check my mouth (and the rest of me), they write down that I'm thirteen. I saw. (I can read their numbers just as well as ours even though it looks all scratchy.) I sure popped from eleven to thirteen in a hurry.

They've put me in a stall by myself, but from what I could see on the way in, most of the others of us are in stalls of four or even more. There *is* another person alone, though, right across from me. A nothing sort of Sue. For sure a nothing. I'm getting good at telling types. She tried to talk to me when they first shut me in, but I wouldn't.

If this really is prison, I like it. A lot. They know us well enough to make us a really good place. They always try to make things nice for us. There's one of those glowy strips all along one side of the ceiling. (You can look right at those and it never hurts your eyes. Hoots' eyes are more sensitive than ours, so they need them like this even more than we do.) There's a soft bed with a soft green cover. There's a folding table. There's a toilet at the back. No window, but on one wall there's a great big picture of an arena, flags flying. All colors. It's more exciting than a window could ever be—unless it looked out right over an arena just as big as this one, and it was the same breezy sunny day with clouds in the background.

I sit on the one and only chair (it has a green cushion that matches the bed cover) and admire everything. I wish I could be in that arena right now with the flags flapping. I think how civilized it all is and how fun and exciting. After that I look at my legs and think how nice they are, even with the scars, and then I think about how I'm growing.

I wish there was a mirror.

I tense my leg muscles. That Sue across from me will see my good legs. Hers are neither Tennessee nor Seattle.

"Hey," the nothing says . . . again. "Hey, hi." But who wants to talk to a nothing?

"Won't you talk? Or can't you? I know lots can't. Just give me some sign."

I turn my back and feel for my mustache. No doubt about it, it's coming along.

"I have a book."

I don't answer. I'm having a good-enough time without one.

"Stories from a long time ago. It's got airplanes and trains. I'll give it to you. I've read it so often I know it by heart."

I wouldn't mind reading about trains and airplanes. I hardly know what they are, but what I'm worrying about now is, is she going to have a good view of every single thing I do? There's only a yard or so of hallway between her white wires and mine. Even if I was at the farthest wall and she at her farthest wall,

I'd still only be maybe ten yards away, at the most.

Well, it depends on how long I'm going to be here—I mean, about whether I'll let her give me her book or not.

"Lots with as many scars as you have can't talk, but they can whistle or hum tunes that mean things."

Nobody ever taught me the whistle talk, but even if I knew it, I wouldn't whistle for her. She doesn't matter. I can say whatever I feel like. Lies or anything. But I could shock her the most with the truth. I could say, "I saved my Hoot host's life and my own father poled me. My father! Top-to-bottom. And my Hoot is . . . ." But I wouldn't tell her who he really is. She can tell all she needs to know about me just by looking. After all, I have my shiny red shorts, my silks, and my silver surcingle. Maybe not the best hairdo, but pretty good. Close as she is, she can't see that half of it is false.

This is a good time to study the etched leaping Sams on the sides of the bit, so I do that. (I took my bit and headstall off right away.) I wonder if she can see those leaping Sams on the sides from where she is?

But it's such a nice, civilized, cushiony chair I fall asleep. Except I still have that collar around my neck with the lead rope attached. The collar is thick stiff leather, and it rubs on my neck and half-wakes me up off and on, but I'm so tired I just go back to sleep.

Another reason to have a mirror is, I could see how rubbed I'm getting.

I have no way of knowing time. The light doesn't change. I don't know long I slept. It seemed long, but it could have been ten minutes. I go drink. Nice cold water right in my stall like there's supposed to be—hot water, too.

I look at the stall across from me. She's asleep now. Sprawled on the cot. Her shoes are off, and I can see her feet are not Wild feet any more than mine are. They're clean and soft. Smaller than any Seattle's, Sam *or* Sue. And narrow. I kind of like how they look. Her hairdo, too, it's not much of one, but nice. I think Merry Mary had one like that, two braids wound around to the back of her head, and a butterfly pin. This nothing has a butterfly pin that reminds me of my mom's. I wonder what she thinks of my hair? We fixed it up as best we could. It has a nice shape to it, lacquered, with painted half-circles at my temples.

She's wearing a silky kind of top. (Not as nice as my silks, though. Mine are yellow and purple with two white stripes. Hers are just plain blue.) I can see everything about her breasts. That top is so soft I can even see the little dip where her belly button is. Up at the village everybody wore thicker things.

Breasts make me think about what it means to be a human being . . . what my father asked but didn't give me any answers to. Was he thinking Wild or Tame? And do Wilds have the same kind of breasts as Tames? (Us Seattles usually have big ones.) Makes me wonder, what about penises?

My father would say we're all human beings. But it's as if he thinks we also have to do something about it. I don't know what that is.

But right now I think being a real human is being right here in a nice, cool prison and eating fresh-baked dry cakes and drinking milk for breakfast. If this *is* breakfast. It feels like it. I don't even know how those dry cakes got here. And there's oranges. Two of them. I haven't had those lately. What it means to be a *civilized* human being . . . *that's* the real question, and, prison or not, this is it. The only bad thing about it is her.

When I slept she could have been watching me like I watched her. There's no way to keep her from it. All I have on are these short, short shorts, and my shirt is silky, too. Mostly what she'd see about me is muscles.

I guess I must be rattling around with my food, because she wakes and sees me watching her. I turn away too late, but when I turn back, she's still staring.

She says, "I wish you'd talk." And then I see tears in her eyes. They just pop out and drip down her cheeks, and she doesn't wipe at them. She doesn't even lick them when they get to her lips. You'd think they'd tickle. I should say something. I do feel sorry for her, but I feel frozen. All stiff and odd, as if—being so close to her like this, and getting watched, and the toilet right behind—I have to keep my dignity.

Then she says, "I'm going to give you this book anyway. I'm sorry about your scars. I know you can't talk. I don't mind. Really. You don't have to try for me."

She puts the book outside her stall and shoves it as far towards my stall as she can. I could reach it but I don't.

I'm thinking how Merry Mary never said anything about being a real human being. What she always said was: Be fair, and honest, and kind, and polite, and I've mostly always tried. She said, *especially* a Seattle should be that way, because not everybody can be as strong or as big or as important as us Seattles, but right now I'm not being a single one of those things she said to be.

I don't know what my father meant because I couldn't not be human if I tried, except I *do* know I'm not being the way a Seattle should be. Especially to another Sam or Sue who isn't lucky enough to be one.

"Did they hurt you? Your neck is all red under your collar."

But the way she looks at me . . . I'm still feeling all stiff and funny.

"My Sue name is Mistaken. I was a mistake. Hoots call me Missy."

Even though I could see she was a mistake the minute I saw her, I don't like that she has to be named that. I finally do shake my head. A couple of big, slow nos.

"But my mother named me Lily."

I say, "Lily." Except it comes out like my father would have said it. "Li. . . ." Long wait, then, "Ly." I don't know if I meant to do that or if it happened by itself. My mouth does feel odd after a whole day with that bit.

"You *can* talk."

But I don't want to risk any more words. I'm getting to be like my father. Besides, I might yodel by mistake.

She's looking at me, squinting as if I need to be thought about. "Are you a Wild or a Tame? I can't tell for sure. You're dressed Tame, but there's things Wild about you, too. Just nod if you're a Wild?"

I don't know what to answer. I suppose I've gotten to be a little bit Wild, even though I never wanted to be. But how do you nod half a nod?

"I know you're special. I know you're not just anybody."

Everybody who knows anything at all can see that.

Then I think about her looks and how she's probably what my sister will be like, lumpy nose, too-high forehead, pale eyes—I can't see what color, they're just too pale. Maybe kind of greenish or just plain gray. My sister might be exactly like this.

"I wouldn't . . . wouldn't. . . ." Why am I talking like my father? That won't keep my voice yodeling all over anyway. " . . . wouldn't like being . . . called Mistaken."

"I'm used to it. Besides, it's always Missy. And besides, it's true. And kind of funny. But I like being Lily. Though I guess I don't look much *like* a lily. Maybe dandelion. . . . No, there's a raggedy kind of aster that always looks as if it's lost half its petals . . . Engleman Aster. That's like me. Call me Engleman."

She laughs—as if being a nothing doesn't matter that much.

"I have a sister. She's. . . ." (I almost say, a nothing.) "She's . . . like you."

"How do you know? I could have a dozen sisters and not know about a single one, and I haven't seen my mother since they took me away."

"I haven't seen my mother, either—not since I was taken, but I was supposed to see her, except I'm here instead."

"Well, what are you, Wild or Tame? And thank you. For talking. I haven't talked to any of us for a long time, except our stall cleaner."

I'm not sure I want to talk to a stall cleaner. Except I'm talking to Lily.

"I'm a Tame." I lean towards the bars and pull my upper lip up to show my brand under it. "But I was with the Wilds for a while. They know things like mothers and sisters. They would even know about *your* mother and sisters."

"Could be brothers," she says, and laughs again. It sure doesn't take much to make her laugh. She's looking at me in that steady-on way again. "I have some cream for your neck. Can you reach through?"

"Do you ever know what time it is in here?"

"They don't want us to know things like that. Sometimes Blue Bob, that stall cleaner, tells me, but then more time goes by and I lose track again."

Just as she's about to give me that cream, along comes a Sam with a bad limp. *Very* bad! His leg kind of drags behind him in a twisted way. I can't look. I don't want to think about it. A completely useless Sam. Not only that, but a completely useless *Seattle* Sam! He's leaning over so much he's not up to his regular height at all, but you can see he was a big one.

He's cleaning with a vacuum thing. He can hardly even do that. He uses it partly as a cane. That book is still lying in the hallway between us. "Book," he says, not quite as badly as my father would have said it, picks it up, and reads the title out loud. "*When Our Land Was Our Land.*" He starts to hand it to her, says, "L . . . Lily. Lily." Twice for no reason even though he can't say *L*s very well.

"It's for him."

"Ah, the mount . . . *the* mount of His Excellent Excellency, The-Ruler-Of-Us-All."

"Lily goes, "Oh . . . oh . . . ," and covers her mouth with her hand—as well she should.

The crippled Seattle gives me this long, long stare. (I'm getting tired of being stared at all the time.) Then he nods and says, "I know that face." He speaks slowly, but clearer than my father. "I *know* that face." When you can't talk that well, you shouldn't keep repeating things. " . . . that same face, but older and sadder." (He should have said, I know that nose.) "5584, guards' mounts. My friend. My partner. Always. I was 5585. We were as if hitched together. Always the two of us out in front because we were the biggest and looked so much alike."

He reaches right in and grabs me by the wrist. (I was standing so close because I was about to reach for the cream and the book. I do want them.)

"Heron's child! I'd know you anywhere!"

I snatch my hand back. He pulls his away, too, just as fast, backs off, and hunches over more than ever.

I turn my back so fast I trip on my dangling lead rope and give my neck a real jerk. How could this absolutely, *absolutely* lame, useless Sam grab for my wrist like that?

Lily reaches out and calls him. "Blue Bob. Bob."

"It's all right."

"It's not! He. . . . You stuck-up nothing! What's your name? I want to know so as not to call you by mistake."

That Bob says, again, "It's all right. He didn't mean to."

Except I did.

"You have to mean the things you do."

That nothing called me nothing. She knows what I am and she still calls me a nothing.

She says, "I don't need your name. When I say Nothing, or Nobody, you'll know who I mean. Except I can't imagine why I would be calling you, anyway."

I don't care. She doesn't matter. I could see that the minute I saw her.

I go to the farthest wall and look at the picture of the arena and all those flags. That picture's about me, not them. I'm the one used to be always down in the middle winning little statues of myself for the Hoots to put in their niches and getting ribbons for the Hoots to hang on their walls. Well, I wasn't old enough for any real races. To tell the truth, I was only in two little practice races.

From the corner of my eye, I see they're holding hands.

She says, "Put the book next to his stall, anyway. We don't want to be *anything* like him."

"Yes, but. . . . Dear Lily, we are. You shouldn't call him a nothing right in front of him."

"I'll say I'm sorry. Maybe. Later. Maybe."

I can hear everything they're saying, and they know it.

"His father was the nicest Sam you'd ever meet."

Why do I have to have such a noticeable face? Everything was fine a few minutes ago, when she was the nobody, not me. Anyway, *they* can't make me feel bad. They don't matter.

Chapter Twelve

A half a day later a Hoot comes. He rolls right into my stall. He's not afraid of me at all, but even though they know I'm a Tame, he has a little crop pole handy. He rolls in on a fancy, filigreed stool with a pink cushion. He's dressed pretty much like a guard, only fancier, with a lacy collar and silky leg hiders. (They love our legs so much, and they don't like their own skinny ones, so they often hide theirs under loose, split skirts.) First he takes off my lead rope and collar and clicks a kind of cluck, cluck, because of how my neck looks. He has scar paint with him, though.

He brought me a fancy clean outfit. I suppose I'll have to dress right in front of Lily, but why would I care?

Except . . . first he shaves me! I've been waiting and waiting for this mustache to amount to something, and he shaves off what little there is of it. I know better than to protest. If I do, they'll know I'm not completely a Tame and well-trained. For Little Master's sake, I have to pretend to be. Besides, that's all I ever wanted to be anyway.

The Hoot harnesses me up, bit and all. Then, "Squat," he says, "Near side." Never in my whole life have I ever had a Hoot on me that isn't Little Master. I'm so stunned I don't know what to do. I hesitate, and then I pull away, but he jerks the bit—hard. It hurts a lot. I think about my father and how he almost had a fit when I put that stick in my mouth and how he didn't want anything like that near me. For him it must have been like this all the time. No wonder. . . . No wonder a lot of things.

I can't stand any more jerking on the bit. I taste my own blood. I squat.

But it turns out that he's better on my bit than Little Master ever got to be, though he tried hard. This host is used to it. He doesn't put any weight on my mouth at all.

"Go," he says. "Gently go. Through the door and to the right. Down the ramp. Then to the left. At the top of the hill, you will turn left again. You will follow the way to the igloo with the golden flags. You will trust in me, my steady, as a steady should. You will be knowing how I will keep you safe. Begin." He gives me a strawberry. I almost forgot about those treats. Then he gives a gentle starting-up pressure with his legs on my chest.

Lily and I look at each other just as I leave. She looks as if she cares about me and worries about me even after all the things she (and I) said. She makes a motion as if to say, "Take care." I wish I dared to motion back. I wish I could say some nice last thing.

I'm so upset I can't remember anything he said, but his legs tell me which way to go, and he looks in the directions so I know. Makes me remember the happy old days (I didn't even

know how happy I was), and how our trainer used to yell at
Little Master, "Look! Look where you're going!" After, Little
Master would slip me a secret treat, sometimes a strawberry,
too, sometimes a bite of ginger candy.

I *was* smiley back then.

We enter the igloo with the golden flags. It doesn't have a long,
low entrance, and it's not even a little bit underground. The
doors are so big we go in just as we are, him mounted, and
inside, every Hoot is mounted. Inside I don't have to lean over.
No danger any of us Sams or Sues throwing up in here. I've
never seen anything like it. I didn't even know there could be a
place like this. It's almost as big as an arena inside.

At first I can't take it in: The shiny white walls, the scarves
and banners, every host in shiny whites, and every mount with
shiny, black, lacquered hair. Light strips are all across the
ceiling. . . . It's a wonderful place. Has my father ever seen it?
Or anything like it? If he did, he'd change his mind. I'm even
changing my mind. No, it's that my mind is even more than
ever the way it usually is.

Then I see Little Master. I can't believe it. He's mounted on
the shoulders of a different Seattle! But I'm right here. I'm *here!*
I guess I must have made some kind of move, because my host
jerks the bit—one of those flick-of-the-wrist little jerks. Little
Master never did that. Of course I never had a bit in any real
way till now. I feel helpless . . . hopeless, too.

There are mounts that are always traded off from one Hoot
to another, they're used to it, but that's never the way with us
best ones. What does it mean to be a very special mount and

not to have my own very special Hoot? And why would Little Master have to ride another when I'm here? I was waiting and waiting and waiting. Just for him.

I can't see. It's too shiny. Even Little Master is too shiny, and he has a look in his eyes. . . . I don't know what it means. A grownup look. A self-important look. He raises his head and looks down his nose—his still-flattish baby nose—at me.

The bright ceiling lights make the Hoots' big eyes glisten. Little Master's starey stare seems to flash out at me.

He's mounted on an absolutely *grand* Seattle. Big as my father (by now I know big as that is rare), muscles all over, and greased all over so he glistens. He has a lacquered hairdo that sticks up and out. He has a perfect nose.

I can't stop looking at that mount. He's where I'm supposed to be. Aren't I big enough, or what? Did I get to be too much a Wild and too scarred and thin? Or maybe it *is* my nose that's all wrong. I knew it. I always knew this would happen.

Next to Little Master is The Magnificent, Munificent Present-Ruler-Of-Us-All. Not mounted, so he's way below all the other Hoots, but there's space around him, and he's on a little platform so I and everybody can see him. This time he's wearing fine clothes and jewels, but he's taking everything off . . . slowly, one thing at a time. He starts with bracelets and earrings and headbands.

"Has it?" The-Present-Ruler-Of-Us-All says. "Has it . . . has, oh, has? And all too soon? Yet, or, one hopes, not yet? And yet all? And still? So that the present . . ." He's talking to other Hoots, not to any of us. They always simplify for us. "So that the present is a time gone by already?"

He's standing up on his little legs, no stool at all. He's wobbling a lot. I think for sure he'll fall. I think to go help him, but nobody else does, so I guess it isn't supposed to be done. Besides, my rider (I don't even know his *name!*) keeps a gentle pressure on the bit.

I hear Little Master say, in a grownup Hoot voice with lots of grownup Hoot resonance, "It has."

By now The-Present-Ruler-Of-Us-All has taken everything off. He's completely, absolutely naked. I've never seen that in a grownup Hoot. And I've gotten used to Little Master's stronger legs. This-Present-Ruler-Of-Us-All . . . his legs are like strings, but his arms are strong. There's a sex bud that I think means he's a mother, but I'm not sure. They tell that sort of thing about each other by other ways, smell mostly, but also the way the voice resonates. Songs, too, because there are songs only sung by mothers.

"I could have wished you to say no," The-Present-Ruler-Of-Us-All says, "Yet a few more times or even once more a no, so as to bring us more slowly into the future."

"It is now," says Little Master.

"Is it you, this odd and other one of us, already ready to take a place that has not yet nor ever been taken in our time?"

"Yes," says Little Master.

"I smell it," says The-Present-Ruler, and, "So is this already the year of the beginning?"

"Yes," says Little Master.

I'm proud of him all over again, how he holds himself, looking up and out. I straighten myself, too, so as to match him. I wonder if any of them notice and remember we belong together—that mine ought to be the shoulders he sits upon.

"Kindness has always been our policy," The-Present-Ruler says. "If it is to come about, we turn (as Sams and Sues might say) our other cheeks. Not swarm and die in clusters, but for the sake of kindness. Let be. Time enough for another policy at some later date."

Then he turns away from Little Master and waves his hand to all us mounts. "You primates were the best we ever had. But we will take care of you as always. We made this promise to you from the start. We saw your legs and said to ourselves, 'These new and precious creatures must be preserved and cherished as we preserve and cherish every part of our very selves.' You are our hearts' desire."

I'm thinking, *yes!* Yes to being fed and taken care of! And yes, we are the best. Even back on the Hoots' own home planet, they had none better. This is not the first time they've told us that. Even Little Master, Future-Ruler-Of-Us-All, said it, his arms around my neck, his breath in my ear. And many times.

"Listen!" The-Present-Ruler-Of-Us-All says. "The *naked* truth as we all, and even you mounts, know it. See me vulnerable and helpless. More helpless than even the least of the smallest of you. Smell! Look! It's your world. Now we give it back to you."

I *knew* it! I *knew* they'd do the kind and caring thing. I wish my father could be here to see how kindness is the best policy, not voting.

All of a sudden there's a tearing, banging racket, and a shower of glittery stucco comes down all over us. A large part of one wall of the igloo collapses, and there stands *us . . . our* army of scraggly, unkempt Sams and Sues . . . not a single decent hairdo among them, not a single shiny white—except where pieces of stucco fell on them, hats, either stolen or handmade. None match. Nothing matches . . . handknit vests, leggings. . . . Some of the surcingles . . . belts, that is, are just ropes.

And here's my father, right out in front, looking the worst and Wildest of them all. I'm ashamed of having anything to do with him—or with any of us.

I yell, "No! Not *now!*" and get my bit jerked again. I want to lean over with the pain, but I can't, because my host holds the reins too tight and has his legs braced around me so as to hold me straight. I have to keep standing at attention. My yelling was lost in all the tearing-down noises anyway.

Then it's suddenly quiet. Something about The-Present-Ruler-Of-Us-All, there, completely naked, and everybody around him standing so still, makes the Sams and Sues stand quietly, too. As they should. Everybody sees how important this is, even us Wilds.

But The Munificent, Magnanimous Present-Ruler-Of-Us-All *is* munificent . . . magnanimous . . . even with half his igloo fallen down around him. He says, "Come in. There's no need to stand there like that, all in rows." He raises his head and bares his neck, ready to receive the leap-and-choke again. He looks grand, even though naked, and even though in the most vulnerable pose there is for a Hoot to make (or us, too). His voice is high and fluty. It sings out both in a grand way and a soothing, cooing way.

"This is the right place and the right time. Come in. And

welcome. We have given over. Here are the keys to the food cabinets. You may eat. And the keys to the arena and the flags. You may race."

He raises his hands as if to give keys, though there's nothing in them.

"Out of the kindness in our hearts, as you know us to be kind, we have given all to you. We have no thoughts for ourselves, but think only of what's best for you. When have we ever not done so? Please. Enter."

Nobody moves.

"Enter."

Nobody moves. Neither us nor them.

I chew on my bit. It makes a little metal-on-metal sound. I taste my blood.

I see everything so clearly: My father, glistening, but I know with sweat, not oil, hair plastered to his forehead. . . .

Time goes by. I'm thinking I can feel it, the way Hoots talk of time, as a thing you can touch and see and smell.

What if *I* spoke out? What if *I* accepted for us all? Yes! And so fast my host wouldn't be able to stop me until it was too late?

I yell it, then. "Yes! We accept." And get another painful jerk on the bit.

But Little Master shouts . . . it's more like singing. A "Nooooooo!" A long, long "No" that resonates, echoes . . . and even when it dies away it seems to hang there. (How do they *do* that? I've lived with him all this time and never understood it.)

If nobody moved before, they certainly don't now, not with that big No hanging there. Why did he say no? What does he mean by that? I've completely lost track of whose side either of us is supposed to be on.

My father sees me then, with the Hoot on me and maybe blood on my lips. (I keep licking at it, trying to keep myself cleaned up.) He goes crazy . . . even more than usual. He looks as if he knows who that Hoot is. He leaps towards me. No man that big could leap that high, but he does. Guards are on him right away . . . and, as always happens, their mounts' boots trample him. Could be by mistake, except those guards are bad. But I only see the beginning of it.

Suddenly fireballs are all around. Flashes from both sides, and a great whoosh of flame, mostly out the broken ceiling and up into the sky. Our fireballs are drawn up—sucked up with those of the Hoots'—so mostly harmless. And our army . . . milling around and not doing anything useful.

I'm closer to The-Present-Ruler-Of-Us-All, and there he is with his neck still stretched out on purpose to look vulnerable. But he gave a signal at the same time as he pretended to give up. I saw it. I think I saw it. Not every one of us Sams would see that, but I've lived with Little Master too long and too closely (lived with, not just trained with) not to know a lot of extra things about Hoots.

I buck. I've never done that in my life before. I hardly even know how. I lean and twist and jump. I use my hands, too. I pull him off me. I spit out the bit. He's a good rider, but I get rid of him.

Then I leap, too, to help my father. Even as I'm leaping, I think: Why am I helping? I know it's hopeless.

Chapter Thirteen

Next thing I know, I don't know anything. And then somebody's calling me who doesn't know my name. Calling: "Young Sam. Young Seattle. Are you all right? Beautiful young Seattle. . . ."

Is it me they mean? In spite of my scars and my nose?

I try to move, but everything hurts.

"Are you all right? I'm sorry I called you a nothing. You're not, and you never will be."

The bed is soft. All around me everything is a nice green. I shut my eyes and try to think.

"Are you hurt? Beautiful Seattle?"

I turn over and open my eyes again, and there it is, the arena, right in front of me, all shiny and bright. At first I think it's real. I think I must have collapsed after a race. They'll say I'm too young. They'll say I'll have to wait till next year before I can race again or I might permanently hurt myself.

I jump up fast to show I'm all right. And fall flat on my face. But there's a rug.

Somebody says, "Wait. Lie still. Please."

I look over and see the thin white bars. I'm right back where I started, and there's the mistake, Lily, across from me, saying, "Please." I can't believe how glad I am to see her.

I sit up, and right away I see I'm hobbled. I'll only be able to take tiny steps, or maybe just hop. This is the scariest thing that ever happened to me. Ever! I'll be a nothing. I'll be like that Bob who cleans up—as worthless as he is. A mistake just as much as Lily. I start to shake.

I try to say something, but my lips are stiff and my mouth is sore inside. All I get out is two whats: "What? What?"

"You've got blood on your lips."

I get up and start jumping towards the sink. I'm dizzy, and jumping doesn't help. I have to stop and sit on the bed.

"Wait," Lily says again. "The blood doesn't matter. I'm sorry I mentioned it."

I lean over with my head on my knees and sit like that for a while. I don't even know what happened. And what about my father? I was going to help him. I didn't even have a chance to do something brave.

"I wish I could do something to help you. What can I do?"

I finally manage to get my mouth around some words. "There isn't. . . ." And then, "Nothing." Then I say, "But my father?"

"Bob knows. He always knows everything. He'll be here. Don't worry."

And there he is. I just have time to jump little jumps over to the sink to wash my face and rinse out my mouth and he's here, shuffling along, dragging his leg, leaning on his vacuum. He's hurrying as fast as he can and he comes straight to me.

First he sees me: He laughs. It's a big man's laugh—like my father would laugh if he ever laughed. It's not a cripple's laugh. He shakes his fists over his head. I know that means well done, but I don't know what for. First I think maybe he's happy that somebody is worse off than he is.

He says, "I know you don't want me to reach in to you, but I'd like to shake your hand." He grabs his own fist with his other hand and shakes that—out towards me.

This time I almost wish he would reach in, except I feel as if I might cry if anybody touched me in a nice way.

"What happened? I don't know what."

"You bucked him off! The champion rider of the batch! You bucked him. When we set our minds to it, we can get rid of them. And you're not even a grownup heavy. I told your father about it. He went down before he saw it. And he's not dead yet."

What does *that* mean? From what I saw, everybody jumping on him, he's got to be hurt. I thought I wouldn't care, but I do.

"Here, he sent you things."

He takes a bundle out of the vacuum and hands it to me. I open it and spread it out on the bed, and here's my father's knife, back to me again, and the belt to hold it, and a handknit vest, but it's not old one, it's his. Here's oranges, and apples, and a cup of black raspberries. Where did he get all this fruit? Was he saving his own food for me again? And there's a note: *My dear . . . my dear, <u>dear</u> son. . . .* The third "dear" underlined. I can't read it now. I put it back with the other things.

This prison is odd. Bob's just the cleaner and can hardly even walk, but he seems to be able to do most anything. Maybe it's another proof of the Hoot's kindness. They let him be in charge, or let him think he is.

That vacuum of his must work even when it's full of secret things. I wonder what else is in there?

"All this stuff!"

"I guess he wanted to give you things and didn't know what. I guess he gave you everything he had. Except his underwear."

(It's always Lily who laughs. What does she have to laugh about, especially being what she is?)

"How come they let you give me my knife?"

"Let . . . they don't let, but I get things around. News, too. We know just about everything there is to know right here in prison. We have ways. Even though we don't escape, nothing escapes us. Put your legs over by the bars. I can loosen those hobbles a little bit."

His hands are rough and calloused like my father's, but he's gentle. He's a lot like my father, except for being crippled . . . except for being a little better-looking because his nose is broken (if I said that out loud, Lily would laugh) and he talks better.

"Your father and I, we were a team . . . the two biggest of the guards' mounts." He already told me, or, rather, Lily, but I don't mind. I want to hear it all again. "Even when we had time off in the pens, we'd stay together. Hoots—and everybody— thought we were brothers."

He shows me how to make it look as if I'm still just as hobbled as before, and yet I can unwind one side one turn.

"You'll be able to trot almost as good as ever."

I breathe out a whole lot of big breaths without meaning to, as if I've been running.

"Feel better?"

I just nod.

"I thought you would. I'll bet you figured you'd be as bad off as I am. That would be pretty scary."

When he's through, he gives my leg a squeeze just the way my father would have done. I have to turn away. When he sees that, he holds on to my leg all the harder. My father would have done that, too. "It's all right. Even we guards' mounts. . . . Back when we were mounts . . . your father and I. . . . We couldn't talk much, but we could cry." He gives my leg another squeeze. "How's your mouth?"

I don't answer. I'm waiting for him to go.

"Your father's mouth was permanently damaged, but don't worry, you'll be able to talk fine."

I shake my head yes.

He stares at me. I know he knows I'm going to cry. Finally he says, "I have to go." Finally he does.

I flop completely over, my face flat in the rug, and I do cry. Even right as I'm doing it, I'm wondering, when have I ever cried like this before? Not since Merry Mary. She wouldn't let go and I wouldn't, either. Did the Hoots really, really have to pole her that hard? I didn't want to lose her, except I'm glad I have Little Master. I cry more then, because of maybe having lost him, too—maybe forever. He's so changed. He yelled, No, just when I was yelling, Yes.

Finally I stop. I turn over. That big picture of the arena just makes me feel worse.

"Young Seattle. Beautiful young Seattle."

But I have scars, and my nose has been growing, and my hairdo is, almost all of it, phony, and I can just barely trot. . . .

"Here. Take this."

I look over at her cage. What she wants to give me is her butterfly hair clip. I sit up. I wipe my nose and cheeks on a piece of the wrapping from the things my father gave me. Her hair clip looks like my mom's.

"That's a Sue kind of thing."

"Take it anyway. It's pretty. You can give it to your Suefriend."

I go close to the bars and take it. It *is* pretty, shiny blue with little red and gold lines in it, tiny yellow eyes made of two tiny, shiny stones. Even the underside is pretty.

"Thank you, but I'll just borrow it for a little while. I'll give it back."

"Please keep it."

"I don't have a Suefriend."

"I know your Suefriend has to be a Seattle, and just as good as you are, they wouldn't let you have any other kind, but if I could, I'd want my Samfriend to be like you."

Of course they wouldn't let me. No matter what. And *of course* I'm just the sort of Sam a nothing would want the most of all. Well, every Sue would. But . . . well . . . she keeps being nice to me.

"*You* can be my Suefriend."

She covers her mouth with her hand. She looks as if she's too happy to stand it. Then she reaches both hands out to me and laughs. "I know you don't mean it, and you can't mean it, you're too important, but it's nice of you to say that, anyway."

I reach out, too . . . if we lean way forward against our bars and push against them. . . . They're not really bars, they're that same white ribbon stuff. I suppose they could turn them on and spark us any time they want, but we don't worry about that, we lean and stretch as far as we can. We can't hold hands but we can hold fingers. It feels good to hang on to another person, even a mistake. But we can't stretch out like that for long, we give up after a couple of minutes.

"I do mean it. Things are changing. Everything's going to be different. We can't go backwards. It's too late for that." I sound just like my father. In fact it's his words, word for word. "There's lots more of us than of them, now. And I saw our airplanes. They flew right over us."

She says, "Airplanes!" and covers her mouth with her hands again, both of them this time, as if to hide her grin. I never saw such a smiley person.

"Smiley is my Hoot name, but you're the one should be called that. You smile the biggest smiles I ever saw."

I like how pleased she always is. I like how I feel when I see her laughing. I even kind of like her looks, even though I know she's ugly. I even like how she's *not* just like me. If I don't watch out, I'll love all wrong, the same way my father does.

For a minute I think I could give her that bit with the silver cheek-pieces, but then I think how, even though it's beautiful, and the leaping Sams at the sides look just like me, I'm not sure she'd like it. I'm not sure she should like it.

"I wish I had something to give to you. I mean besides giving this back later on."

"I don't even know your name . . . your person name. All I

know is Bob said, Heron's child, and now I know your Hoot name is Smiley."

"I'm Charley."

Then I make her take some of the fruit my father gave me. At first she won't, but I say we'll sit on the floor close to our bars and have a picnic together. So we do, but the fruit stings the inside of my mouth. I yell at the first bite, and she grabs for my hand again, except now it's my turn to have my hands around my jaw.

"Poor beautiful Seattle, you're going to get even thinner. People will think you're a Tennessee."

We laugh, because of course they won't. Seattles are all tall and have black hair. (If it isn't naturally black, it's dyed.) And Tennessees have either reddish hair and freckles like Jane, or they're blond. Jane is a pretty good specimen for what she's supposed to be. I wouldn't admit that before, even to myself . . . *especially* not to myself.

"I'm sorry I wouldn't talk to you before. You're the first. . . ." I won't ever say *nothing* anymore. "You're the first one like you I ever really was this close to." There were plenty up at the village but I made a point of not getting close to them.

"When would a Seattle as special as you are have the privilege of being next to a big mistake?"

She always sounds as if she doesn't care that she's nothing but a mistake.

"*Little* mistake. Besides, you're nice and I really do want you for my Suefriend. I wish I had something of my own to give you."

The apple doesn't sting my mouth so badly. I can eat it if I cut it into little pieces with my knife and don't chew much, but I can only eat a little. I sort of pretend so as to keep Lily company at our picnic, but she can tell.

"When the milk comes, I'll give you mine. I'll ask Blue Bob to bring you something you can eat. You could soak your dry cakes in milk."

"Yauwch."

After we eat, I sit back on the bed and look at the butterfly hair clip again. It looks civilized and artistic. Delicate. Sometimes it's nice to have a Sue kind of thing for a little while.

Then I remember my father's letter. I unfold it again.

My dear . . . my dear, dear son. . . .

I guess he means it. Even just that part makes me feel tearful again. Last I saw him, he was at the bottom of a pile of guards and mounts. All Bob said was, "He's not dead yet." I don't know what that means. I should have asked. I guess I was too scared about myself being hobbled. My legs are the most important part of my conformation. Lots of Hoots say they look at the legs first and don't much care about the rest.

I hang on to the butterfly clip and read.

I put a burden on you when I came for you. I knew people would expect things from you as they do from me, but I feared, if I didn't get to you in time, you would rebel and be put in solitary and then made a mount to the guards and pitted against your own people. I trampled my own mother. I can hardly write it.

I wasn't being fair. I wanted you to think like me, be like me, do as I do.

But Little Master, walking! That's a whole new thing. There's a solution I haven't thought about.

The way you and Little Master are together! That's entirely new. Hoots <u>talk</u> *of kindness and caring, but you two have come to it. Your relationship is not mount to host but friend to friend.*

Odd to have his writing be so smooth. I guess I expected it to be the way he talked.

You once told me kindness is better than voting. I should have listened. I trust you and Little Master to find the way.

Love, your father.

Sometimes . . . *often* I used to think: Well, how does he know he's my father, anyway? I was hoping he wasn't. But I know it's true, he really is.

Lily and I eat every meal sitting on the floor next to our bars, as close to each other as we can get. I have the book now. Well, we both have it. Sometimes she reads to me, and I lie on my cot and listen. She has a nice voice. Every now and then she says something ridiculous as she reads. For a minute I think it's really in the book, but then I know it's another one of her jokes. I don't read out loud to her because it still feels funny to talk. Almost as if some nerves won't work anymore. Yodeling and cracking is the least of my worries now. My voice is the one thing Lily doesn't ever make jokes about.

I never really did know what trains were until this book. Lily says the tracks are still here, though a lot have been removed for the metal. Lily says by us. She says we're making a lot of important things out of them. Maybe those airplanes and bicycles.

Lily saw some tracks once. They went on as far as she could see in both directions. I told her about those little red flowers as far as you can see in every direction there is. She never saw that.

Mostly I tell her about the village. She loves to hear about that the best of anything. She thinks she'd like it even if there isn't any easy-to-get hot water and you have to make your own clothes. And shoes—and they don't last very long. I tell her about my father's having strings hanging off of his. Hats made out of leaves or grasses or leather unless you can steal them.

"Nobody cares about racing up there. That's the *least* important thing. You could have bowed legs or knock-knees and nobody would care." I don't say how bad that makes me feel, because I know it makes her feel good. "Nobody's a mistake, everybody's all mixed up. You can love anybody you feel like. And there's a lot of different things to be. You could knit or sew or cook or plant things. People would appreciate all of it."

"It sounds as if, up there, you won't have to worry about being too thin for being a good Seattle."

"If eating hurts this much all the time, I guess I won't get any fatter."

I explain voting. She thinks she'd like it, because even if you lost, you'd have had a say, because they talk it over.

"A lot," I say. "They talk and talk, a lot more than you'd want."

"But I'd have one whole vote even if I'm just a mistake . . . one whole vote! You'd only have one, too." That makes her grin again as if the joke's on me. And it is. (Actually, it did seem as if my father had more votes, though that wasn't supposed to happen. And I didn't seem to have any.)

"I know I *am* just a mistake, but you said, up there, being a good mount and racing and conformation aren't the one and only things, so if they aren't, I could win ribbons and statues and medals with my cleaning up. Could I? And you said I'd get to keep the ribbons. I'd put them on my own walls. I wouldn't have to give them to any old Hoots."

She gets this dreamy look. "Think of that, prizes for cleaning up. I'd. . . ." Then she laughs so hard she can hardly talk. "Champion scrubber."

She's so silly, but I don't say that. For all I know, maybe there are medals for that.

"People always talked about what was up in those mountains and I've imagined places like that. I'm not the sort that likes all these comforts anyway. I'd much rather be a real person than have fancy things."

"I'm a real person. I was a real person from the start. Even up there."

"Maybe *you* are, and I know I'll never be as real as you, but I'd like to be a little bit realer than I am."

"You're like my father. He doesn't care for comforts. He likes things hard to do. As long as he can vote, he doesn't care." When I talk about him to Lily, he doesn't seem so bad. "He rescued me, but I didn't want him to."

"I wish somebody would rescue me."

"I'll do it."

That makes her laugh again. If she wasn't already sitting on the floor, she'd fall on it.

"No, *I'll* rescue you."

"It's already been done. That's how I ended up in prison.

But you know, they will rescue us . . . maybe use airplanes. Swoop down right at the prison doors."

"You, maybe."

"Maybe Bob will do it. You'd be first, then."

She says, "Don't laugh, he really might. Bob does more than you'd think."

"I know that."

But I must have made a face, because she asks, "Does it hurt to talk?"

"No, it just feels funny. I'm sorry I wouldn't talk to you when I first came."

"I'm used to that. It happens all the time. People take one look and think, there's the absolutely perfect conformation for a typical nothing, and won't give me the time of day." She looks up at those light bars that are always glowing, night or day. "I wonder what time it is, anyway."

"*I'd* give you the time of day, if I knew."

Chapter Fourteen

Blue Bob comes again, and I ask him right away about my father. He says the same thing, "He's not dead yet," only this time he says it kind of hesitating. This time it's not a joke, and I realize it probably wasn't last time, either.

Then he says, "I'll tell you two a secret." He's avoiding talking about my father. "We wanted to get some of our people in here—in prison. It's part of our plans. But your father lost control of himself."

"He saw me."

"Yes. And we know that Hoot well. He and I hosted him before. Often. Your father couldn't stand to see him riding you."

"Is he all right?"

"Bright Spot . . . Jane is with him."

"He's *not* all right."

"He wants to see you. I came to take you to him. Don't let him see your hobbles."

"You can take me there?"

I guess Bob can do anything. I guess Bob really is in charge. "Lily, you stay."

He holds out what looks like a little three-inch piece of our bars, bends it, and my bars fall into a white clump—into what looks like an impossible tangle. He makes Lily's bars fall, too. We don't even think, we go to each other as if to hug, but then we both stop, and, after a minute, just hold hands.

Bob says, "You've changed," and then, "Come. . . . Charley. . . . Come."

I let go of Lily. I think I'm in love. This must be it.

Bob points with his thumb for Lily to go back in her cell. He bends the little white wire, and the bars untangle themselves and spring up again.

My hobbles are loose the way he showed me. I can keep up with Bob's shuffling, no trouble at all, and I can go up the stairs a lot better then he can. I wonder about the stairs. Usually Hoots don't have indoor places they can't go without stools. They always have ramps. They couldn't come up here without mounting one of us. Little Master could, though.

My father is in a special room. No bars. Jane sits beside him. A thick woolly blanket is pulled up to his chest. It's more like one of the blankets from up in the village than any of the soft, silky ones the Hoots would have. He looks terrible, grayish-green, even with all that red-brown from the sun. Dark circles under his eyes, and his nose seems bigger than usual, a lot. And his face, bonier than ever. He's a lot thinner, too. How did he get so thin so fast? Has it been that long? Can you get that thin in just a week or so?

And then I see. . . . And then I see. . . .

I can't breathe. It's like that time before, blackness closing in from the sides until there's just a little hole of light, only this time I'm not getting choked. I have to sit down. I'm going to throw up. I flop down, so fast I bump my head on the edge of the bed. And then Jane is beside me. "Lie back," she says. She washes my face with the cold water she has there for my father. I can smell him on the towel.

"It's all right." My father whispers it. Then Jane says it, too—louder, as if for him, like she always does when he has trouble speaking.

But it's not all right. My father . . . maybe he's not The-Present-Ruler-Of-Us-All, but he's a Ruler . . . *one* of the rulers of us Sams and Sues. And . . . but. . . . *Legs* are what we live by. They're our main worth. Our only worth. And he's lost a leg.

Practically every other thing that happens seems to be because of me, but I never asked for any of this. I didn't ever want to be rescued. I never even asked to have a father, especially not an important one.

"Jane, is that because of me?"

"Of course not. Why would you say that?"

"Bob said my father got upset because of me."

"That isn't your fault."

My father groans a long, growling groan.

"Am I like Little Master? Am I supposed to take over for my father? I don't know how."

"Charley!" She lifts me so I'm half in her lap. She kisses my forehead. It's as if I was my father. "Oh, dear. What'll we do with him?"

My father reaches down so his hand is on my shoulder. "It's all . . . right. I'm. . . ." He not only can't get his tongue and lips around the words, but he sounds out of breath, too. " . . . in charge. In charge, I . . . Bob and the others. . . ."

Bob squats next to us. "*I'm* in charge," he says. "Couldn't you see that?"

Then my father sees my feet. All of a sudden he's got the strength to sit up. He starts to get out of bed. He's as afraid of my hobbles as I was, and yet he's lost a whole leg.

"Get those things off him."

His voice is, all of a sudden, so strong.

Bob jumps up to hold him down. They get into a kind of fight and Bob wins.

My father lies back and groans. It seems like it's more for me than for himself. But what are hobbles compared to no leg at all? No leg *ever*?

I push Jane away and shuffle myself to the sink, and I do throw up. I didn't want her to, but Jane comes and holds my forehead. After, I collapse again, on the floor by the sink.

Nobody says much for a long time. Bob and Jane just sit there. Jane beside me, and Bob, his arm on my father's shoulder as if still holding my father down just in case he tries to get up again. My father closes his eyes every now and then, but mostly he watches me. Stares. I never did like it when he did that, but I don't mind it so much now. Then he starts talking nonsense. He can't get his mouth around the words. I know how that feels now . . . exactly.

He's getting upset. "Kindness *is* . . . that which. . . ." Groan. "What . . . *what!*" and then, "Bright Spot. Bright, Bright . . . Spot."

Jane leans over, her arm across his shoulders. "I'm here, and Charley's here. He's all right. *Charley's all right.*"

I would have liked to hear what he wanted to say about what kindness is.

Jane says, "Kiss him," and I do, on his cheek, but I don't think he even knows it. He feels greasy, and he smells funny.

Bob hangs on to my arm all the way back, as if he thinks I'm going to try to run away. I hadn't thought of it till he held me so tight, but where would I go? And I wouldn't want to be anywhere without Little Master. I don't even want to think about myself out somewhere alone. Could we both escape? Where *is* Little Master? How could I find him?

But I don't ask Bob that. I ask him how my father lost his leg. He says, "Those poles can cut you in two when they're turned up." Then I ask him why my father cares so much about me. "He goes crazy every time he sees me in trouble. He'd rather my hobbles were off than have his leg back."

"One of these days, you'll understand."

I hate when people say that. Do they think I'm still a child? I'd have a mustache by now if they hadn't shaved me. Besides, it's just an excuse not to tell me things.

But then he does go on. "Heron and I had terrible, *terrible* times, both of us. Have you any idea how it feels to have spikes inside your mouth all day long? Have you any idea what solitary is like for herd animals like primates?"

"But he goes off by himself all the time—as if he can't stand people anymore."

"I think sometimes he can't stand himself. That's what

makes him do that. I don't know, he's. . . . But about you, I think. . . . He had nothing and never had anybody. . . . And then you're so like him. When he saves you, he's saving himself."

He's not finishing half the things he starts to say, but I don't ask any more.

As soon as I get back in my cell, I start to shake. I try to tell Lily about my father, but I can't. I can't get any farther than the word "leg." We reach out and hold tips of fingers. Lily has tears in her eyes, too, just from seeing tears in mine. I *am* in love. I hang on to her fingers for as long as I can stand the reaching.

Little Master comes. Finally! He dismounts halfway down the hall and walks in on his own. He doesn't wobble at all anymore. He's even better at it than before. For sure he's been practicing by himself. Lily can't believe it. Her eyes look big as Hoots' eyes. Of course, not that big, but sort of.

He sends his mount away. I guess he knows how I feel about seeing him anywhere near a different Sam, let alone *on* one. He clicks down the bars. They fall in a scramble, and he comes in—*struts* in. He doesn't look at all like Hoots do when they try to walk. They always lean forward with their big hands out to the sides for balance. He perches on the edge of my cot, lifts his legs and hugs his knees. Compared to our legs, his are thin and short for his body, but they look like real legs now, not strings.

He's got a ring or two on each finger and three or four earrings up and down his ears. He makes a little jingling sound when he moves. It's going to be hard for him to stroke or pat with all those rings on.

I'm so stunned to see him here, and all in new, shiny whites, I don't know what to do. I say, "You, you, you," like the Hoots always do.

And he says, "Me," which they hardly ever say. And then, after a minute while we just look at each other, he says, "I heard about your father."

Then he sees my hobbles. He looks almost as shocked as my father was . . . as *I* was, though I'm pretty used to them now, and I've gotten used to hopping myself around. I'm pretty good at it.

For a minute he can't say anything. Then: "My sturdy. My steady." His ears flop down beside his cheeks.

Tears come to my eyes, too, partly because I thought . . . well, I knew he couldn't have, but I wasn't sure if he'd forgotten all about me. But I'm not . . . not, not, *not*, going to fall on the rug again and spend the whole afternoon like I did before.

I sit on the cot beside him. We sit close . . . touching. . . . Just sit. He looks as if he wants to give me a lick or some pats, but he doesn't.

Finally I say, "I thought you'd left me for good."

"*Never!* I've learned all about your primate love. In one lesson. It's what I feel for you."

I say, "I feel that, too."

Then his ears perk up, straight up and towards me. "You bucked him off!"

He's as happy about it as Bob was.

"Whose side are you on?"

"Yours and mine. No other. Only yours and mine."

"But when you said no, to my yes? What was that about?"

"They were trying to make you think they'd given over. They always do that, give up and give over. Like The-Recently-Past-Ruler-Of-Us-All said, the doors of the treats and the doors of the arenas. They knew you'd like to keep racing. (You would, too. You're like us in that.) They'd let you oversee the races and run in them, even let you keep your prizes for yourself, but it would just look like freedom."

"How come you know so much about it?"

"I was there with your father, too, remember? I listened. He didn't convince you, but he convinced me. He was right about false freedoms. He wanted to open the doors of all the land, not just the doors of the snacks, but it's going to be hard to tell when and if they surrender. That's why I was yelling no."

"Even the way you talk is more like us Sams and Sues than a Hoot."

"I'm half of one thing. Without you, I'm only half. Even though I can walk on my own, I'm still just a part. You're just half, too, you know, can't hear, can't smell, can't see all the way around."

"You don't have to tell me."

"Don't be angry."

"I'm not." To prove it, I show him the butterfly hair clip and introduce Lily, which I forgot to do before. "She's a somebody. She's my Suefriend."

He looks at me as if he's about to say, "That's the wrong kind of love and against the law." I can see it on his face, but before he can say it, I say, "Things have changed."

"You have, too."

"I never knew one of the . . . one of them. Never really knew one of those, before Lily."

"Now that I'm The-Present-Ruler-Of-Us-All . . . Munificent, Magnanimous. . . ."

"Are you? Really? Already? That's wonderful."

"It's a trick—like everything they do. Without trickery they'd never have gotten anywhere."

"But kindness has always been the Hoots' best policy. Maybe it's kindness made him give over to you."

"Of course . . . of *course* we Hoots are always kind, and we want all our Sues and Sams to be healthy and comfortable, just look at this prison, except. . . . I don't know what kindness is anymore. You can't leave things out. Like give half a kindness."

"I don't mind half a kindness."

"Half a kindness is what we've been giving you primates all along."

"I like it that way."

"That's not what your father likes."

Lily has been quiet all this time, as if, like most of us, she's a little worried about a Hoot being right in here with me, but now she says, "Half a kindness? I only got about an eighth of a kindness, if that. Once I got poled because I went to help an old Sue they were poling. I was the kind one." She's just like me when I tried to help Sunrise.

Lily said she worked in the lettuce patches on the hottest days and got heat stroke lots more than once. This is what my baby sister will have to go through unless things change. I never did think much about babies, but I'd kind of like to see what my sister looks like. She could even look like me, just not breed true, is all. They don't always have to look like Lily, halfway between just about everything. But it's odd how I've gotten used to Lily. I like how she looks.

"The-Recently-Past-Ruler-Of-Us-All could be ruling me, and I wouldn't even know it," Little Master says. "Remember when he and I went back alone into that cubby? Number one, he said Hoots can never turn burrows over to Sams and Sues, and not even domes, because most of you can't stand to be in them. You throw up. (That's true. And I heard that you *did* throw up.) Number two, he said did you Sams and Sues want us all to kill ourselves? Number three, he said we can't live without you, but I told him we can. I said, 'Look at me,' and I ran around the cubby, and not just once or twice. Ran! Then he said, 'Who will clean and cook and work the fields? Lower primates can't do it. We tried that a long time ago.' But *I* cleaned. Remember? Up at the village? When you had to clean, I did, too. I helped with everything you had to do. We planted things together. You, then me, then you, then me, then you. I liked it. I told him that.

"Number four, he said he might be my mother. Most probably was, depending on which womb of the seven that might have held me.

"I will see eye-to-eye with your father, not with my mother. Mine has been naked ever since he took off his clothes. He gave me all his jewels. It's supposed to be a sign. I told him I take my signs and signals from you. I didn't tell him about the airplanes, but I told him you had secrets."

"What I want is the freedom to love," I say. It just pops out by itself, and I feel embarrassed afterwards. It looks like I embarrassed Lily, too.

"That's what I want," Little Master says. "And for the two of us, trotting over the mountains, eating berries, stepping aside for rattlesnakes, sleeping curled up together as if womb mates. . . . What if we went right now?"

I guess I'm not as civilized as I thought I was, because that's exactly what I want. He'd be my eyes and ears and nose, my sense of time and place and bad weather coming.

"Can you get us out of here? We'll take Lily. I promised her I'd take her to the village. We'll pick up your doll on the way and my mom's picture."

Now Little Master's ears are swiveling all over the place forwards and back, and Lily looks just as happy.

"I'll bring the butterfly," I say, "And my father's letter."

Then the white wires spring back in place all by themselves. I guess somebody hears everything we say. Or maybe they listen because Little Master is here. I guess Blue Bob isn't the only one in charge.

Little Master's ears droop. "There," he says. "I told you. I can't do a single thing I really want." He sounds like a baby again.

"It's nice that you're in here with me, though."

"I wonder when they're going to let me out?"

"Stay."

"I can't be much help in here."

It doesn't take long. I'd have liked it longer and so would he. It's just like what happened with Sunrise, first the ring of metal heels on the cement floor of the hall, three guards on their big Seattle mounts. Their eyes are starey like my father's. They look beyond us, as if they don't want to see what they're doing. That's what gives them that crazy look they all have.

I'm just standing there, and they push me and pole me anyway. Lily is yelling, "Stop!" But Little Master is squatting on the bed in the leap-and-choke pose, and nobody, not even the Hoot guards, dares to get close to him. Those strong legs of his make him look entirely different from any other Hoot. Nobody knows how far he can leap now. I don't even know myself.

"You will back off," Little Master says. "You will leave this Sam alone. You will bring my mount, and I will come willingly, but you will not hurt this Sam and this Sue."

Usually his talk is more like us than Hoots, but not this time.

They back off. The mount comes . . . another slicked-up champion Seattle, of course. Little Master gives me a look. He doesn't dare show anything, and I don't, either. He quits his leap-and-choke pose, takes off one of his earrings and one of his rings, and throws them on my bed, then says, "Go, go, go," and they go.

When they're gone, Lily says, "He's the best of them I ever saw."

I take the earring he threw on the bed. It's a long, dangly one of a leaping mount. Little Master knows how much I like those. I hand it and the ring to Lily. "Now I have something to give you."

"He wanted you to have those, and he's your special friend."

"How about then I keep the butterfly clip for a while and you keep these for a while. Does the ring fit? Their fingers are so long and thin."

But it does. Hers are thin, too.

She says she'll wear the earring on a string around her wrist so she can see it. "It looks exactly like you."

Bob comes back. He makes the white wires fall and shuffles himself right in and sits on my bed. He can't look at me. He leans over, elbows on knees, hands over his face. It's bad news. He can't tell me, but I guess it.

I sit beside him, not too close, but he moves over and grabs me, hard, clutches my head to his chest, holds me too tight, and starts to cry. Why do these big, strong Seattles cry all the time? I don't know what to feel. I never do when this happens. I just have to wait till they stop. I don't feel anything. Except squeezed. Then I think, but I *need* my father. Then I think, do I have to do something? And what is it? Is everything up to me now? And then I think, I can't do it.

After a while, Bob lets me go. "So," he says, "it's done." Then he looks at me, as if it's a question. I don't know what he needs for me to be saying. If I'm supposed to cry, I can't do it right now. I'm not doing anything right, but he's not doing things right, either, because he hasn't even told me my father's dead. What if he isn't? What if he's just lost his other leg? Or maybe it's somebody else that's dead.

"If I just had my legs back in shape. If only . . . if only. . . ." He stops right in the middle for about a whole minute, then, "My mother always told me there's no such thing as, if only."

He and my father are so old and so big you wouldn't think they'd ever be remembering their mothers.

"Your father was. . . . There's no one like him. *You* will be, but now there's no one." He turns away and collapses over on my bed, his head right on my pillow. But at least he's not holding me this time. I hope he'll stop crying pretty soon. I can't think when he does that. I can't even really realize my father's dead.

"Poor Jane. . . ," he says. "She's having a baby. Maybe one like you."

Not another baby. And how could a Tennessee have one like me? And even if it looks like me, it would be like my sister. It would never breed true.

Chapter Fifteen

It's time for a talk—one of those heart-to-heart talks (that's what *they* call it) the Hoots always give, with strawberries, one by one, the little sweet kind. And lots of pats. And, "Have I considered my future?" or, "Have I considered their side of the question?" kinds of things.

Right after Bob stumbles out, the Hoot comes. I don't have a minute to think about anything. He rolls in on a fancy stool. He has a short crop pole. He rolls himself over to my only good chair—where I am.

At first Lily looks as if she hardly dares move, but then she gets off her bed and moves her chair close to her bars and sits.

"You, my favorite," the Hoot says. "My sturdy. My steady." He holds out a strawberry, but I don't let him put it directly into my mouth. I take it with my fingers. Of course, maybe I shouldn't let him give me any treats at all, but I don't think about that until I've already taken it.

He leans his head back and actually bares his neck to me. I'm tempted, but he'd be faster with his leap-and-choke back at me, even with his neck like this. His legs are braced around the legs of the stool, as if ready. Maybe that's what he wants me to do, so he can finish me off.

I think this might be the same Hoot I bucked off and that my father and Bob hate so much. He *is* dressed in a head guards' uniform, and he has champion ribbons. I should stop taking treats. But I haven't had strawberries for a long time.

"Remember when you were little?" he says. (Strawberry. Strawberry.) "How we came every month with new toys? We patted you and fed you treats by hand? Remember? And your mother sat beside you, and patted you, too, so you wouldn't get upset? And there was chocolate. Just like this," and he hands me one of those little one-bites called Kisses, wrapped up in foil. I put it behind me into the chair cushion to save for Lily.

I do remember, and I remember I was always glad to see them. That's when I got the name Smiley.

He says, "There's only one question and only one answer. Do you want to live life as a Wild or as a Tame? A civilized *champion* primate? With plenty of the proper food . . ." (Strawberry. Strawberry.) " . . . so you'll grow to your full size and strength? Look at yourself. You're so thin. Much too thin for one of your type. You must eat and train.

"But, as of now, all new rules with you in mind." (Strawberry.) "As of this morning, you . . . all of you can mate with whoever you wish. You can take charge of the arenas. You can take charge of your stalls. There will be no solitary and no bits, even for the most intractable of you. You may speak."

I don't.

"None more loved than you champions. You know that. We sacrifice every day for you. Did and still do."

Another chocolate Kiss.

I get up and pace (well, not exactly pace with these hobbles on, more shuffle) from my sink to the bars. I can't sit still.

I say, "His Excellency The-Ruler-of-Us-All wasn't fooled by you."

If I could come up from behind him? Of course that's impossible. There's no sneaking up on a creature with prey eyes, but what if Lily could make a loud noise? I turn towards her and try to give a signal, hidden by my body, but she doesn't understand it.

"The-Ruler-Of-Us-All is being retrained."

I trust Little Master. He might pretend to be retrained, but he won't change the side he's on, which is my side.

The Hoot's head isn't moving, but he's watching me, because one ear faces me as I circle.

"You killed my father."

"He brought death upon himself. Death is always up to you. You know that."

"He was tortured. Spiked bits for years at a time. He was driven crazy. *You* did it."

"Only those prone to craziness are driven crazy. Your father was brought up in the best of circumstances, just like you were. Everything was done for him that could be done. He won every race. Until suddenly he refused all hosts. Like you, he bucked. He was utterly useless until he came to us to be a guards' mount. The spiked bit changed his mind . . . and a little while in solitary."

All of a sudden I'm going to burst. I'm sweating. I can hardly breathe. I know exactly what my father felt when he went crazy. I'll risk anything. I don't care. I have to do something.

I've shuffled around to his back. I'm moving slowly, slower and slower. His ear points at me. He knows exactly where I am. I know he can smell my rage. I just hope he can't see how much I'm shaking.

It won't work. Nothing I do can be as fast as he is, but I don't care.

Except Lily does make a noise. She drops her wash basin on the tiles of her sink area. It clatters so loud it even hurts *my* ears. The Hoot spooks right off his stool. Flops on the floor. Before he can get back up, I grab his neck from behind. I shake him and shake him. He tries to get his hands around behind to me, but I keep shaking him. It works. He wasn't ready.

I don't know if I killed him or not. I don't wait to find out. I use the white wire he used and make our bars fall. We run, as best I can with hobbles, right past the Sam the Hoot rode in on. He's standing at parade rest, waiting. He doesn't move as we go by. I can't tell his expression, his big black mustache hides his mouth, but he raises his eyebrows, then gives a tiny half-wink.

I pull Lily past the front door—she tries to get away and out, but I'm stronger. I pull her past another front door and then up the stairs to the room where my father was.

I hadn't thought to go there, I just go. I don't know why, except where would we head if we'd gone outside? I'd just hobble along and get caught. This seemed safest. And maybe the Hoots will think we've gone out. That's the logical thing to do. There's white wires all around the whole prison that would have stopped us, anyway.

I think I also had the idea my father would be up here (nobody *really* said he was dead) and all I had to do was get to him and everything would be all right. He'd know what to do next.

But the room is empty. The cot where my father lay is rumpled. The blanket pulled aside. You can see where his sweat dried all over it. You can see where his head was on the pillow. There's a bad, sick smell. Like there was before, only worse.

I lose all the angry energy I had. I collapse on the floor, like I did before, when I saw my father'd lost his leg.

Everything is not going to be all right. And whatever we do now, we have to decide it all by ourselves.

Lily gets cold water at the sink for me like Jane did. I watch her walk across the room, and, for the first time, I get a really good look at her legs. She's pigeon-toed. Nobody bothered to put her in braces, when she was little, to fix it. Nobody cared. I'm getting angry all over again. I slap the floor with my fist and hurt myself. Which is exactly something my father would have done. Lily jumps back, scared of me.

I'm so angry I hardly know what I'm saying or why. Things just pop out. "I know I'm too young for any of that stuff now, but Lily, will you marry me? When I'm old enough? I don't know the rules. I don't even know how old that would be, and I don't even know how old I am."

"You're asking that *now!*" She laughs, like she always does, no matter what or when, and then she says, "Of course I will."

Then I have my first kiss. A lover's kind of kiss. It's maybe the wrong place and time, or maybe we need practice, because it doesn't feel like much. But Lily looks at me, after, like it doesn't matter how it was.

I think to try that kissing again, but we're interrupted by noises outside. There's only one little window, and we kneel down by it, holding hands, and look out.

Here we are: My father just dead, and I don't have Little Master, and I don't have any idea what to do next, but with Lily and me free . . . sort of free and together, I don't feel as bad as I ought to feel.

Outside there's Hoots all over. Some of the mounts are kneeling so the Hoots can sniff the ground, other mounts are trotting around, and the Hoots are lifting their heads and sniffing the air. Hoots' ears are twisting all around. It won't take them long to realize we're still in here, but they won't know where in here. The bad smell from my father is masking our smell.

We watch for a while, and then we look around to see what's in the room, which is less even than in our cells downstairs. There's some spoiled milk. (Lily's about to throw it out, but I say, "This and my father's blankets might come in handy to mask our smells." Lily says, "Phew, I hope not.") There's a container of dry cakes that's never been opened.

We don't feel like sitting on the bed or touching it, and there's only one straight-backed chair, the one Jane sat in next to my father, so we go to the window—the air is fresher there—and sit on the floor. We hold hands. Ever since we got free, we're holding hands just about all the time. She leans her head on my shoulder so her nobody-nothing hair is against my cheek. It's straight and neither yellow nor brown and not much shine. I don't care. Who would want everything to be the same? Except I used to.

"I forgot your butterfly clip."

"But look, I still have your earring."

"I forgot the chocolate I saved for you. I feel like going back for it."

"Oh Charley, please don't. If you do, I'll never kiss you again."

"I like your hair. Even without the clip."

"Who ever heard of a Seattle liking hair like this?"

We sit. I sneak my hand around to feel how breasts feel. She lets me.

After a while she says, "What should we do now?"

"Maybe we can open all the cells and let everybody out."

"Bob could do that. I wonder where he is? Maybe he'll come and find us. Maybe we should wait till things calm down. Look outside, there's a lot fewer Hoots out there now. Look . . . only four."

I lean towards her to look, and then, without planning to, I practice kissing again. And I practice kissing her cheeks and her neck. And she practices the same on me. Afterwards, we both say, "You," and, "You," and then we laugh because we sound so much like Hoots.

I keep wondering how come I can feel so happy when for all I know we'll be thrown into different cells far from each other and never see each other again.

One thing, though, I know how my father felt about Jane, and I know how that rage felt, how he didn't care about anything when he got angry. I wish he was here so I could tell him

I understand. I guess my feelings show, because Lily says, "What's the matter?" and I say, "I was thinking about my father, how I never said anything nice to him. Not even once. Not *ever!*" Then I lie face-down on the floor again, this time Lily cuddling up beside me just as Little Master used to do. I feel bad, but not as bad as I would if she wasn't here.

Lily keeps saying, "He knew. He must have known."

"Except for Jane, I was what he cared about the most. I don't even know why he did, because I was never nice to him."

"If he cared so much about you, he understood."

"At least I kissed him—even though he smelled bad, I kissed him—but I don't think he even knew I did it. He was out of his head."

"Maybe he did know. Maybe his body knew in some body kind of way."

It's getting dark. We hear whistling. It's mostly coming from in the prison. It's a friendly sound, us calling out to us.

"Do you know what they're signaling?" Lily knows more about those things than I do.

"That last was 'Bye Bye Blackbird,' but I don't know why. That song makes me so sad. I don't know why *that* either."

Then somebody right below us in the prison plays a sort of ukelele kind of thing and taps on something and sings without words.

Lily pigeon-toes over to get the dry cakes and a cup of water. There's only this one cup. It's just a plain white cup. I hold it out to look at it. I say, "My father drank out of this."

"Then drink," Lily says.

We sit by the window and listen. The song stops and the whistlings get to be few and far between, soft and slow. There are lots of other night sounds, bugs and such, and a cool breeze is blowing in. Everything is so nice and everything is awful and scary, too.

I take out my father's knife (I've been wearing it under my shorts) and start working on my hobbles. After a while, Lily works on them, too. We finally cut through.

Afterwards we lean together, and then I ask Lily what I've not thought to ask all this time.

"Why were you locked in here? What did you do? It couldn't have been such a bad thing."

"It *was* bad. I worked in food. I. . . ." First she can't say it, and then she does, all in one bunch. "I poisoned an important Sam. A Tennessee. A champion. He was. . . . I didn't matter, he mattered. I made him sick. I didn't kill him, I just tried to. First they put me in solitary, but not for long. I liked it because it got me away from him. Then they brought me here. Blue Bob says I've been here about a year."

"How can you be such a smiley person? You laugh all the time."

"I like prison. They didn't even pole me. They don't kill, you know, at least not straight out. They didn't know what to do with me—except give me a talking-to every now and then. Blue Bob looked after me. I was never as happy as I was here. Bob brought me treats and books. He brought me my butterfly hair clip. He was the nicest to me anybody ever was. Better than my mother. She was a Tennessee. She had good feet, not like mine, but she never had much speed. She might have had some good offspring, but after me they gave up on her. I ruined what little status she had. I got to stay with her longer than most because I wasn't important enough to be taken away for any kind of training. I never even got imprinted. I don't know what that's like. I always wondered."

"It's like this," I say, and stroke her neck and shoulder. I put my finger in her ears and in her mouth. I move her arm and hand wherever I want them to be. "All this and more," I say, and touch her breast again. "In fact, no place is left out, but I'll leave out some." Then I kiss her neck.

"You silly."

"I wonder, even more, how come you're such a smiley person?"

Then I wonder if there's a comb around here. I want to comb her hair and put that hair clip in it. Which I don't even have.

"What's wrong now?"

"I'm thinking about your hair clip."

We spend the night cuddled up together just as if she was my Little Master.

Chapter Sixteen

First thing in the morning, there's a loud crackling, spitting sound. It's got to be the white wires—all sparking at once. I'm still half-asleep. Even so, I know what it is. I worry about all of us down in the cells below. I dream we've all lost our legs, and then I think, if none of us had legs, everybody'd be crawling around on their bellies, and we wouldn't have to be mounts. Then I think how that would be just the way my father wanted it, every creature equal, like he always said. Then I wake up all the way, and I think, more likely everybody in prison is dead now, except for us up here.

I realize (for the ten thousandth time) how much I depend on Little Master to hear and smell and tell me what's going on. He'd know. He can even smell if a death is new or old. By myself, and with just Lily, I can't tell anything.

Lily and I hold each other and wait and listen. I can feel how Lily is all stiff. It's like hugging a bundle of sticks. I guess I'm like that, too.

Then we hear the sounds of us outside our window. (We're

quiet out there, but you can hear soft talking.) More and more of us. We jump up to look, and there we are. The prison bars must have dropped, all at the same time, and the prison front doors opened, and here we are, coming out. It's a big prison even if it's mostly only one-story high. It goes on and on, curling back and forth in a snaky shape.

Our kind is wandering around looking dazed, wondering what to do. Like, is this the revolution right now, or what? And if it is, what are we supposed to do? They need somebody like my father to start them off. I have a good, big, booming voice. I could lead. I'll bet they'd follow. But where to? Maybe it doesn't matter. We'd just go. I can see it, everybody behind me, and me trotting out pretty fast—me with my mustache and my silks. My father didn't want to lead, but he did it anyway. I do. I want to.

Here come the Hoots. Mounted. I thought maybe they wouldn't be anymore, especially if they let everybody out, but how would they get here if not on us? They'd just crawl around not far from their burrows. They always say, "If not for you, we'd have to duck into a hole and freeze up and wait or die." And that's true.

The Hoots come trotting—all in rows and all dressed up. I think again how good they look and how I'd like to be one of those Sams they're mounted on, going tramp, tramp, tramp with their metal-soled boots, but then I remember that I really wouldn't like it.

Except these Sams have their bits and headstalls hanging around their necks, as if for everyone to see how free they are and how they must have chosen this job. I *would* like it if I could choose to be there and no bit.

Behind the Hoots there's a little bunch of us—six of us marching together, and with our primate kind of instruments. I'd like to be part of that, too, but I don't know how to play anything. They wouldn't let me learn things like that because I'm a racing Seattle and too important. They all stop, and then the musicians begin to play. Their instruments are brassy and shiny, and the sound is brassy and shiny, too. (Not a Hoot kind of sound.) The sun is just coming up from behind the hills. They were all in shadow, and then suddenly—well, *sort* of suddenly—the sun pops around the jagged part of the mountain top, and they're in sunshine. The music stops.

There's silence, except you can hear birds. The instruments shine out as if they were the mirrors we signaled with up in the village. Somebody must have timed it to be exactly this way. That's a Hoot kind of thing. They're always into art and beauty. And they wouldn't have had to figure it out, they could have smelled the time the sun comes up.

Lily is so impressed she gives a loud, "Ooooh." All of us down there do, too, but the Hoots don't. Every Hoot looks up at our window, but none of us do. The Hoots hear her even with all those other oooohs going on, which goes to prove, *again*, that my kind can hardly hear or smell or see *anything*. Of course they already knew we were up here. They'd have seen us if we'd moved at all. (Little Master always said even if we just move our eyeballs, they'd have seen us.)

All of us below are watching those in the sun glitter and shine. (Our kind stops and watches things like this, too, but it's such a Hoot kind of thing to do. Even though they always talk about not wasting valuable time, they never think art and beauty is a waste of time.)

Then I see Blue Bob. He's right under our window, close to the wall. He's not looking at the sunrise. He's looking out at everybody else, arms folded across his chest. He's got his vac-uumer next to him. I wonder what he's got inside it now. I think he knows Lily and I are up here. He might even have checked in on us as we slept. Without Little Master to see and hear, we never would have noticed.

After the sun has come up enough to shine on all of us, a fancy Hoot rides out in front. This one is still using a bit. The cheek-pieces are of gold on top of silver, and in that pattern I love the most of any. If I had a bit like that, I might want to use it, too. For a few minutes he keeps his Sam trotting in place. It looks so impressive when they do that. And sounds impressive, too. I wish the whole bunch were doing it.

I see his little finger of the hand on the reins twitch, and the Sam stands still, at first at attention, then there's another little finger twitch, and it's parade rest. (Those are not Hoot things, we've always had that, and we've always had racing silks just like these, too.)

"None more loved than you," the Hoot says. It's in the cooing-of-a-mother tone of voice. Lily and I hold each other even tighter. We feel loved, and loving, too.

"You are free. All of you. Free. Go." His arms are out now, his fingers spread. "To the east, to the west, and so forth and so forth, until you are all at a place of your own desire. You will go. You will choose."

Nobody moves.

"Go. It is as you've always wished. Go someplace."

Nobody moves.

"Or you are free to live here in prison, which is your prison now." He pauses. It's a long pause, then, "You may speak."

No one does.

He raises one arm up and then across his chest. "The same gesture that rejects, accepts," he says. "The words that tricked become the words of truth."

Another pause. He expects something of us—for one of us to say something. Who would do it? If not me?

"We bear our throats to you," he says. "As you, on the other hand, would bow, offering the back of your necks." And his head *is* raised so his neck is vulnerable.

"There will be, if you wish it, things that glint and glitter. As cut diamonds. Their smell is the smell of time and of deep places, their facets are the facets of the light itself. Many other things will be given, such as racing shoes. Those of you who host us at this very moment, have been given, as well as many tidbits, racing silks, hats, and replicas of themselves in gold."

I'd like nice, new racing shoes just about more than anything I can think of, and if they gave them to everybody, wouldn't that be as democratic as a thing could be? There's no need to vote on it. Everybody would want them.

But somebody ought to *do* something. My father would. Here's Blue Bob right here and he's not saying a word. Why isn't anybody saying things?

I know I don't know much, but I have a voice that sounds

out. People pay attention. I could say thank you, and we do want shoes.

Except Little Master said it was all a trick. I have to remember and not get tricked.

But thinking gets me all mixed up, and I'm never going to know what freedom means, or even if I like it, or even what it's *for.* When have I ever been free? *Especially* I wasn't, up in what they called the free village. Besides, did my father think *at all* when he jumped that big jump to try and save me?

I yell.

Bob is reaching up towards me already. I jump. Down into his arms. It's as if we'd planned it. It's as if I'm my father, the Sam who rides avalanches.

It was already pretty quiet except for the Hoot's voice singing out, high and sweet. Now it's just me, and my voice isn't sweet. It's raw and rough and it yodels right in the middle. I'll bet I'm scary.

All us Sams and Sues, and the Hoots, too, gasp when they see me jump and hear me.

When I land, I'm halfway as if mounted on Bob. Two Seattles, one on top of the other. I'm the highest of anybody. This feels exactly like when my father carried me and Little Master all the way up, across the pass and down the other side. And just as I felt with my father back then, I can feel how strong Bob is, even still.

I stop yelling, but everybody's still listening. Then I say what my father said. "Hoots are here to stay."

The Hoots coo at me, and this time my kind doesn't yell no, and shake their fists, like they did up in the village. Even so, I yell, "They are, they are. But it's *us* who should be saying what we'll give to *them*. If they like shoes, *we'll* give shoes." That's a dumb thing to say (what Hoot would need shoes? Except maybe they will someday). "If they like gold, *we'll* give gold. It's *us* who will be kind. We'll have the tidbits. It's us who'll imprint *their* babies."

But then I hear a long, loud, Hootish "Hoooo," and then long, loud "No, no, nos," and then I hear everybody catch their breath again, us and them, too.

I should have known. Of course it's Little Master. Who else would be saying I'm all wrong? He's trotting in on his own. His hoing doesn't hurt our ears, but any louder and it would. I lean over when he gets close to me and reach down. He grabs my hand, climbs up Blue Bob, and mounts me. He yells out, "We'll *all* have shoes. We'll *all* have diamonds. We'll imprint each other. This mount and I have already done it."

At first I don't know what he means, and then I realize that's exactly what we did do.

I say, "This is my true friend."

My kind doesn't yell no at this, either. I suppose that's because most of us here are not incorrigible guards' mounts like the ones at the village, and the ones that maybe are, maybe have started to hope for something different.

But then the Hoots' ears swivel to the right, all of them, all at once, and a second or two later their heads turn and they look up. We do the same. Not because we hear anything, but because they do. Then, finally, and probably last of any creatures on this whole wide world, we finally hear, too. Our airplanes.

The guards' mounts . . . it's as if this is what they were

waiting for . . . they buck and pull at their hosts until all the Hoots are crawling around with nothing to hang onto but each other. They form wobbly clumps of threes and fours. Though they're dressed all fancy, now they look ridiculous. And it *is* chaos, at least for them.

That head Hoot guard, who spoke before, is leaning on two others, trying to stand up, and calling, "My dears. My sturdys. My one-and-onlys. . . ." But nobody is paying attention. "Go. Yes, yes," he says, "but in a different moment and in a different way. Wait. There are other things. . . . Races to be won."

But he gets drowned out. Even he, because all the other Hoots . . . *all* do their hos. We have to lean over and hold our ears. Little Master has his hands on top of my hands to help me hold out the sound.

I'm thinking, no wonder Hoots took over with hardly any killing, though it's a wonder we aren't all deaf. I wonder why we aren't?

When the hos finally . . . *finally* dwindle away, *everybody's* on the ground, us along with them. (Me and Blue Bob, too.) The Hoots are even standing up more than we are since they're leaning against each other. That was a long ho, but I've no idea how long. None of us look very sure of anything. I wonder, did they hear it all the way up in the airplanes?

The head Hoot wobbles up to Bob and me and Little Master. (Little Master is still more or less mounted. He's hanging on to my hair as I get up. That's a baby Hoot thing. It isn't ever done, because what would happen to your hairdo?)

That Hoot is just standing there, as if waiting for me to say something. I'm thinking, do I have to be the one to speak again? It has to be important. But then Bob says, "This is Heron's son, and this is His Excellent Excellency, Present-Ruler-Of-Us-All."

"It is known."

Bob says, "No one can begin the new ways and no one can go on except these two."

"Already known. But we must have mounts. You can see that. What if several new things became the truth, such as: Stalls of many stories the way you used to live, and your racing ribbons on your own walls? What if three or even four of you for one single job, and a say in when and what? What if we, ourselves, would sweep?"

"I've heard your poles are about to lose their power."

"Even the lighting system, the white wires, the warmth. . . . All too soon gone. We knew this time would come. So are we to crawl into our burrows and let our blood run slow as snakes at night?"

"If I were you, I'd learn to walk. Also, we can build you stools that move."

"We accept."

The airplanes are circling. I read about bombs. Except they'd get us and them both. No doubt about it, we're in this together. At least we are right now. Maybe always, like my father said.

Bob says, "We also accept. We will live contented as long as these two are, both of them, Munificent. They're still children, but innocence is called for at a time of new thinking. None of us can think thoughts anything like what these two can think.

And, as you have seen, if one of them says yes, the other will say no."

"We accept."

This time it's Blue Bob who says, "Go. Stay if you like and be mounts out of the goodness of your hearts until we've made motor stools. You'll be well-treated. But the rest of you, get out of here."

He's like my father, if he says go, everybody goes. Some of the guards' mounts help their hosts to mount again. Some of us go back in the prison. When I see that, I think about doing it myself. I did, mostly, like it in there. But then I think how I'd like to go up to the village again. I start away, back towards the mountains, but Little Master leans back in stop position. "Your Suefriend! Listen!"

Then I hear her, too. Up at our window. "Charley," softly, practically a whisper, as if: Who can be expected to be bothered turning back for one like her?

And I *had* forgotten about her. I know her well enough to know it's exactly what she knew would happen. It's a wonder she's even calling out at all. It's a wonder she isn't hunching down, away from the window, making sure we don't remember her.

I yell, "Lily!" I start to run back into the prison, but Bob shouts, "I've got her." He raises his arms just as he did for me. She's scared, I can see it, but she jumps. Her mouth is open. Her hair flies up behind her. I never saw anybody so. . . . She really *is!* It's as if her very nothingness is what makes her beautiful. And how brave she is. That's beautiful, too.

She and Bob stand there hugging. I wish it was me had

caught her. But she might not want to get close when I have Little Master on me. She'll have to get used to him. I'll have to get used to all the Sams and Sues, whichever kind they are. I already have a good start on that.

Later this was said:

For you, then, the Munificent, Magnificent, this gift you have wished for. Several free days in a row to The-Rulers-Of-Our-Voting. You will travel alone and silently. Listening. You will hear the squawk of jays and ravens. You will eat those bitter little berries you have spoken of. You will find the treasures you hid, your doll, and the picture of your mother. There you will greet your mother and your sister and Bright Spot. You will yell out when you come to the yelling-out place where the view comes suddenly upon you. There will be the black mountain on one side and the gray on the other. You will say, "Yes," because you will be happy. By the stream you will make promises, and to Lily, seeing eye-to-eye. You will face the sunrise. It will be just the way your father turned around to see it. And you will say, "Yes, yes, this is as Heron did." Then you will return.

This was said, and we were sent away with new boots and a hat. So for us, then, one more time as if forever on the trails, the two of us—the three of us—up to the village.

Little Master says, "Remember the ruins your father showed you? We could make a landslide in the canyon below them. You could do it. We could live a long, sweet life hidden up there."

"Life isn't just one long thing of the same things one after another."

"It could be."

"We could vote on it. The three of us."

"Oh, but now, how . . . ," he says. "How, right now, we do go. Step me. Trot me. Sing me along the paths. All things are songs. Smells and all, good songs. Even the air is a song. I see our shadow, yours and mine. I see how my hat covers us both. How we do go along seeing new things and old things, too. As if this flower was unlike any of the others even of its own kind. It's as if you also were not of your type, but of yourself, nor I of my type. Go, go, go, now, do go."

We go.